Science Fiction Stories

R.A. Hogan

SCIENCE FICTION STORIES

R.A. HOGAN

Dappled Worlds Press, LLC

Truth is so obscure in these times, and falsehood so established, that unless we love the truth, we cannot know it.
—Blaise Pascal, *Pensées*

CONTENTS

THEY

Alice stood on the ledge brooding over the spectacle. She was told to go there, and she had learned to always do as They commanded. For They were the knowledge keepers, They were the understanders, and They were the all-knowing. The task of keeping humanity safe had been assigned to them in days long since consigned to benightment. The empty, gray sky outside the doorway frightened her. Alice took a deep breath as the supernal fog at her feet churned unabated. They told her it was what she needed to do, but her fearful heart had yet to be soothed. The capricious wind swirled through her hair and under her clothes. She had never felt anything so cold; she had never felt anything so free.

Through the clear sheaths covering her eyes, a menu appeared. Alice blinked, taking a picture with her lenses of the unknown world before her. "This doesn't feel right," she said, uploading the picture. Her words were digitized into the Connection and thousands answered, line after line.

"It is what They command. You will feel better," wrote a friend.

"You can do it!" encouraged another.

"You're so close," said a stranger.

Alice nodded in agreement, yet her heart sank for reasons she did not understand. These were her friends, and they believed she could do it. She thought back in embarrassment to all the times she had been wrong. What a fool she could be. She was nothing without guidance, and now They were telling her to jump.

It all started with the question she made the mistake of sharing. A silly, foolish idea. A thought barely formed before its illumination to the world: "Has anyone ever disconnected?" An innocent curiosity, but the question had ignited even more intrigue than that image of her in a bikini. The mere four words had caused an outpour of anger.

"Of course not, you idiot!"

"It says right here http://www.thebox-world.org/hisory/They."

"LOL u no nuthin."

The question lost her over one thousand followers, and she had been flooded with reprimands from sponsors for the lost revenue. Overpowered by disappointment and resentment, Alice had done the unthinkable. She disconnected. She removed her contact lenses and left her quarters. She hadn't physically ventured out in over five years, and she couldn't recall the last time she talked to someone face-to-face. Last time she left, it was to recalibrate her neural sensors so that her lenses continued to work with her changing brain. She was twenty-two now and was due for another update. Other than neural sensor updates at the clinic, there was never any obligation to leave her living quarters. Everything was delivered to her. In the Connection, there was always something to entertain her. When there wasn't work, there was fun, and plenty of people to talk to.

She shut the door to her quarters and stepped out. The door was drab and metal, not a good representation of the life lived on the other side, where screens filled her walls with exotic worlds and the climate could change to her liking. The world outside her home was a dark and dingy labyrinth of confusing halls and mechanical ductwork, which no one knew much about, other than it helped sustain their way of life. She half-contemplated turning back to the comfort of her living quarters when she spotted a woman approaching.

"Are you lost?" the woman called to her. The stranger moved hypnotically, her thick eyelashes flickering seductively as she got closer.

"I—I'm sorry," responded Alice, wishing she had ordered more from her beauty compact that morning.

"They interrupted my Saturday chat group to tell me to leave my quarters. They assured me there was someone outside I needed to talk to…face-to-face," the woman declared haughtily.

"Well, if it was me, what do They want you to say?" Alice answered.

"Why is it you aren't connected?"

"I don't know, I suppose I just wanted a break." Alice shrugged.

"A break?" said the woman in surprise. "I've never heard of taking breaks from life. You won't make a living if you don't advance your holdings. You must get sponsorship and you must buy what you advertise."

"I've bought all the skin products I can," Alice said.

"You have pleasant skin; I would assume you get paid well for sharing your likeness," said the woman.

Alice was flattered by the woman's unexpected compliment. "My favorite product accredits me for 30% of its sales."

"Who are you?" asked the woman, placing a manicured nail to her lips in contemplation.

"My name is Alice J."

"Well, Alice," said the woman, lowering her voice. "I'm afraid you could be in great danger if you continue your disconnection."

"What do you mean?" Alice said. The woman leaned in close.

"I once had a friend, and, although it was frowned upon, I stayed connected with him purely for his conversation. But soon he had the idea that he wished to be disconnected like you. Then he started getting more ideas and sharing them with the world. He wanted to leave the Connection for good, and he asked me to join," the woman's voice began to shake. "I told him we'd never had it so good. My friend needed to look at the history They have provided. War, hunger, and injustice were once very real. Now no one is hungry. The only wars we have are fought peacefully among advertisements and social forums," she sighed. "But he didn't listen. Instead, he asked me who I thought They were." The woman brushed back her perfect strands of hazel hair. "I haven't heard from him since."

"What happened to him?"

"I don't know," said the woman.

"Do you think he ever got his answer?"

The woman took a step back in disbelief and began shaking her head. "We've never had it so good," she muttered. "I've got to get back. I've already been away too long." The woman rushed away; her silhouette shrunk until it disappeared around a bend. The woman was right. Alice didn't need to disconnect when her entire world could be safely investigated within the privacy of her own walls. Alice shrugged and began to turn back toward her quarters. The door next to her caught her eye, and she stopped.

They

"Britta B.," she read the name on the door. Alice smiled. She had spoken to Britta B. on several occasions and considered her a friend. She shook her head at the unlikelihood that a friend would live so close. Alice had to meet her face-to-face.

"Britta?" she called through the door, knocking happily.

"Yes?" a meek female voice answered.

"It's me, Alice J. Can I come in?" There was a long silence until the door opened, revealing the woman Alice had known from the Connection.

"Ha! You look just like you do in the Connection! Except…Britta, are you pregnant?"

"Alice?" answered Britta, baffled. "How did you get here? We're face-to-face."

"I only live a door down, isn't that crazy?"

"Yes, well. Um, come in, please." Britta looked to the air. "Alice J. is at my door. What are the odds?" Britta said, and her words were filtered to the Connection.

"Your living quarters look almost identical to mine," Alice noted. It was a surprise. Britta's place always seemed to have softer lighting and larger rooms when they talked in the Connection. It never looked like her own quarters.

"Alice…it says you aren't connected right now. Is that true?" asked Britta, an ounce of fear in her voice.

"Yes, I'm not connected," she answered.

"Why?" asked Britta.

"I didn't feel like visiting www.theboxworld.org/history/They," murmured Alice.

"Oh, I saw that," said Britta.

The two sat in awkward silence for a moment, until Alice asked, "How long have you been pregnant?"

7

"It's been about twenty-two weeks," she said. "I ordered it to start a new business venture. You should try it. There are so many advertisements for pregnant women: lotions, belly slings, clothing...the list goes on. It pays well, and when my nine months are up, there are tightening lotion and diet pill ads. Not many do this, so it can be very lucrative. People will buy things even if they aren't pregnant. I'm surprised you didn't notice my ads during our chats."

"I may have, now that I think of it," Alice said, smiling. "I guess I'm just always distracted by your interior living ads. I'm glad for you though." Alice scanned the area, not noticing any of the décor she saw during Britta's chats. In the Connection, Britta's walls were covered in colorful art and her furniture looked lush and cozy. Face-to-face her place was utilitarian and washed out.

"Thanks," said Britta. "The belly is a bit of a hassle, but my virtual encounters haven't taken a hit."

"Would it be weird if I felt your stomach?" asked Alice.

Britta contemplated the question for a moment, and then shrugged. "I don't think so. Go for it," she answered.

Alice knelt down and placed her hands upon her friend's stomach. They both flinched at the unusual feeling of human contact. The surface was firm and warm. She considered what it must feel like to be pregnant, and then suddenly she shot back in surprise. "Something moved," she said.

"I felt it too," answered Britta, eyes wide.

"What moved?"

"Well, I suppose it must be the baby. This is the first time I've felt anything like that."

"So there's a living baby with you all the time?"

"If it moves, does that mean it's alive?"

"I don't know," said Alice as she placed her hand upon her friend's stomach once more.

"Ha, there it is again," whispered Britta.

"I wonder if it can sense that I'm here," said Alice.

"Wouldn't that be something…" Britta said, pausing to inspect her belly.

"Say, Britta, what happens after you have it?"

"They receive it for growth and development."

"You never get to meet your baby?"

"My baby?" uttered Britta. There was silence and Alice watched Britta's eyes move in confusion, before suddenly returning to a state of concentration. "Yes, I understand. I have the same problem. This is what I would do: All you need is a teaspoon of essential oil. Trust me that will help." Britta smiled to the air.

"Britta?" asked Alice. She looked up to her friend, who had essentially forgotten her company.

"Ha, that is so funny. I've never seen anything so funny." Her face changed to a scowl. "Pace T., what is your deal? Get off here." Alice sat back and watched her friend speak to the air. The world of the Connection was still going on without her. Alice wondered what she was missing and a part of her ached to know.

"I guess I better be getting back. I'm sure I've missed a lot." Alice stood and went to the door. She thought she heard Britta whisper a goodbye.

As Alice reentered the hallway to return to her room, she noticed the door directly across from Britta's had the name-plate Pace T. bolted to the door. She recalled Britta saying the name moments ago, so she knocked.

"Hello?" squeaked a man's voice.

"Pace T.? Can I speak with you?" The door slowly opened, and a blue-eyed man peered through the crack. He looked at Alice hesitantly. "Can I come in?"

"Well...who are you?" he asked.

"I'm Alice, Alice J. I was just visiting Britta B. and I heard your name, and on my way out I saw your name on this door. So, I thought I'd meet you."

"Britta B. lives there?" Pace asked, motioning to the door across from his.

"Yeah."

"She just exiled me from her page," Pace growled.

"Why?" asked Alice.

"I tried to sell her a drawing," he mumbled.

"A drawing? Whose drawing?"

"My own."

"You draw?" Alice pondered the man for a few moments. "Can I see?"

Pace's head shot up in surprise. "Do you always visit people face-to-face?"

"You know, I can't remember ever doing it before today," Alice said.

"This would be a first for me," said Pace. "I would like to share my drawings with you, only I'm afraid you won't like them. I've only shown a few people, and no one has liked them."

"I'd still like to see them," she said. Pace backed away from his door and Alice entered. His room was quite different from Alice's. A harsh light beamed from the ceiling. It was unkempt and cluttered with papers; a sweet smell lingered in the air.

"Where did you get all of this paper?"

"I ordered it, and it came," he replied.

"Are these your drawings?"

"Yes," Pace answered nervously. Alice inspected the papers. There was a drawing of a light bulb, one of a bed, and one of a door with light shining through its cracks. "I like this one." She held up the picture of the door.

"You do?" Pace said in astonishment.

"I never realized how the light shines through our doors," she said. Pace smiled bashfully at her approval. "What do you want for it? I'd like to keep it in my room. I live just across from you. I could gather something from my commercial goods."

"Just take it," he said, grinning tearfully. "I don't need anything for it."

"Are you sure?" she asked.

"Your praise is payment enough."

"Thanks," Alice said. She headed for the door, but Pace grasped her arm. The feel of his grip was startling yet somehow pleasing.

"Are you going to meet someone else now?" he asked. "I mean, face-to-face."

"I'm not sure," she said.

"Would you…maybe meet someone for me? I've had dreams of meeting him, but I'm too scared. Could you speak with him face-to-face and tell me what it's like? Meeting you has made me realize that I must—I mean, I have to meet him," he spouted.

"Well, I suppose I could," she said. Pace encircled her in his arms. Alice froze. Pace's embrace was warm and oddly comforting. "What are you doing?"

"Oh," he yelped, releasing her from his hug. "I'm sorry. I was just so excited and felt like holding you." He looked at her in embarrassment.

"It's okay," Alice said. Confusion strained her thoughts. Pace's arms around her had felt comforting and foreign all at once. "What's the name of the man you want me to meet?"

"His name is Nash D."

"Nash D., got it. I will look for his name and return…maybe even with him," said Alice, with a wink.

"Thank you, Alice." Pace blew a breath of relief.

"Is there anything in particular you want me to tell him?"

"I would like to tell him that I love our conversations, and that I would love to meet him face-to-face," Pace said, pausing for a moment. "I don't know how to explain it, but I don't like the days I don't speak with him. The days I get to talk to him are the best. They're the days I feel like drawing."

"Why do you think that is?" she asked.

"I don't know," he said. "But maybe when I meet him face-to-face, I'll know."

"I'll be on my way, then," she said, exiting his quarters.

"Thank you, Alice," she heard Pace say as she ventured down the hall. She held Pace's drawing gingerly as she walked, examining every door for the name Pace had told her to look for, but she could not find it. Alice walked bend after bend until she realized she had no memory of how to get back to Pace's quarters, let alone her own. She began to panic over her fatuity. Her breath caught in her chest as she started to run toward the direction she thought she had been, only to find a bare steel wall blocking her way. She began in a new direction, and for hours she floundered through the endless corridors until she finally spotted a door with the nameplate Nash D. She paused, collecting her thoughts for unanimity a moment before knocking. There was no answer. She knocked again. With her second knock, the door flung open.

"Who are you?" asked a clean-shaven man.

"Oh, uh, I'm Alice…I'm sorry, but I was sent here by a friend of mine," she struggled with her words.

"You were sent here?" he asked suspiciously.

"Yes, by a Pace T.," she said.

"Oh," said the man, frowning.

"He wants to meet you face-to-face," said Alice.

"Then why didn't he come himself?" he asked bluntly.

"He…well, he couldn't," answered Alice.

"I guess I'm just not understanding the concept here," he responded with a flick of the wrist.

"Pace said he enjoys your talks," recited Alice, in a hopeful tone. "And every time he speaks to you, he feels like drawing. And he wanted you to know that the only good days are the days he gets to speak to you."

Nash shook his head with a laugh. "The only good days are the days he gets to speak to me. Is that a drawing of his?" asked Nash.

"Um, yes," she said. Nash took the paper from her hand and inspected it severely.

"This is complete crap. I could draw a better door in the dark, and what are these rays coming from it?" he said, tossing it to the floor. "The only reason I talk to Pace is so he'll buy my products. I sell hair products and colognes. You could use some hair product yourself. I'm looking at five potential buyers as we speak, so if you're not interested you should scram." Nash's eyes went hazy as he focused on his lenses instead of her.

"I don't need anything, thank you," Alice responded. "But I am afraid I'm a bit lost out here. Could you look up directions to my quarters from here?"

"Hold on a second, everyone," announced Nash, as his eyes shifted back to Alice. "You aren't connected?"

"No," she responded.

"And you're lost?" said Nash.

"That is correct," she said.

"That's the most pitiful thing I've ever heard," he said, laughing. "I tell you what, how about you come in, let me finish a few convos, and then I'll show you to your living quarters. In return, you'll need to buy something from me, though." Alice nodded and entered the room, which smelled of thick cologne and other mysterious odors. It was a plain and dark room with neatly stacked items. She waited patiently, listening to Nash speak with eloquence and politeness to his connections. She began to feel a pang of sadness for her earlier life, the life before she had wandered far from her living quarters and away from the Connection. She felt in control while in the Connection, never lost.

"Okay," announced Nash. "We have a few things to talk about."

"What?" Alice asked.

"Alice J.," he uttered as he tapped his fingers upon his neck. "You know, They told me you were coming."

"They did? Why?" she asked.

Nash shrugged and began pacing the room somberly. "They said you must stop visiting just whoever you want. You've already begun to spread the sickness."

"Sickness!" Alice stiffened.

"But They warned me, and They have protected me from the illness, as They protected the first woman you met. But she failed at stopping you. The others you have spoken with are not as lucky. They had no time to protect them because They could not predict your actions." Nash shook his head in disappointment.

"What will happen to Britta and Pace? What will happen to me?"

"They said that you and the others, Britta's baby included, will fall into an inescapable illness, unless They cure you soon."

"What's the cure?" she asked.

"They want you to reconnect and follow directions." As if waiting for his words, a package fell into his drop-off box. Nash opened the handle and reached into the slot in his wall, pulling out a plain white package. He unwrapped the package and handed Alice a small black box, which held a pair of lenses suspended in liquid. "Put them in," he commanded.

Alice looked at the lenses. The world she knew best existed there in the clear, thin sheaths. But there was another world where people could touch, talk face-to-face, and see things for what they were. Britta's apartment had been different than it was in the Connection. Nash acted differently toward her than those he spoke to in the Connection. She hesitated.

"It's the only way, Alice. Don't you want to live?" Nash said.

"Yes," she said.

"Then put them in," Nash said.

"You're sure it's the only way?" Alice asked.

"They say you will die if you do not reconnect," Nash answered. "They will not be able to cure you. A sickness will grow in your brain and take over until you can no longer function in this world."

"I will die? But where did this disease come from?" she asked.

"Please, Alice. No more questions. You've already put the people you've been in contact with in danger. You risk harming others by going on this way," Nash said. "Stop being selfish and do as They say."

Alice nodded. "I need to warn Britta and Pace and tell them I'm sorry." She fingered each lens from its liquid compartment and slowly placed them into her eyes with shaky fingers, blinking until they settled into place. The familiar layout of the Connection appeared before her once more. She rapidly searched for Britta and Pace. "I can't find them anymore. Nash, when did you talk to Pace last?"

"Only a moment ago," he answered.

"Did you warn him?"

"I wrote what They told me to," he replied.

"What did you say?"

"That his artwork is hideous, and that I would never want to meet him face-to-face."

Alice gasped. "Why would you say that? How is that warning him?"

"They said it was the only way to cure him, but besides that, it was the truth," he responded, indifferent.

"That would cure him..." Alice's thoughts raced, as she continued to search her database. "What about Britta? Where is she?"

"Alice, stop worrying. Britta is offline because she's receiving treatments. They will cure her. Now, it's time for you."

Dozens of notifications appeared before Alice's eyes; her counterparts had already heard the news of her illness. "I can't talk!" she shouted into the Connection.

"Alice, you're getting very ill. Look at you, you're sweating." Alice patted her forehead nervously. "You'd better go," Nash declared.

Nodding, she followed the directions transmitted to her. She rushed out of Nash's quarters and through the many curves of the hallways. She finally reached the door she'd been directed to. She opened it, and a brisk wind blew her back.

"What is this?" she shouted.

"KEEP GOING," a message scrolled across her lenses. Slowly her eyes adjusted to her new surroundings. She realized the door was not an entrance to a room, but an exit. An exit away from the world she had known, and the entrance to a world she had never fathomed.

"Where is this!" she cried. The wind hit her face, causing tears to trickle from the edges of her eyes. There was nothing but gray before her and swirling clouds below.

"It is your cure," a voice spoke out loud from the Connection. "Jump."

"Jump? Where does it go?" she yelled.

"To a different place. You are too ill to survive here any longer, but this place has fresh air, and it will sustain you longer."

She squinted, searching for an object to rest her eyes upon, but all she could see was a swirling, thick fog.

"Is it a long drop?" she asked. "Will it hurt?"

"Not at all, Alice," They answered her now. Alice began trembling.

On her lenses, a menu appeared. She took a picture and uploaded it. "This doesn't feel right," she said. The words went off into the Connection and thousands answered line after line.

"It is what They command. You will feel better," wrote a friend.

"You can do it!" encouraged another.

"You're so close," said a stranger.

"Will I be alone in this place?" she asked.

"You will always be connected, Alice," They responded. "You will never be alone."

"I don't want to be without the Connection again," she whispered. "Why did I ever leave?"

"This will remedy your desires," They said.

"If it's for the best," she said, and drawing one final breath, she jumped into the churning fog.

COLFAX COUNTY COAL

The words blurred on the page with the train's erratic rocking. Orange light from oil lamps softly danced across the walls. Edward relented, rubbing his eyes and tossing his book into the empty seat beside him. He turned his attention toward the window; past his own reflection, a nocturnal wasteland emerged. He had heard the area was growing in prosperity, but Edward saw no evidence of it from his seat. Rocks, shrubs, and sand rolled by in the immense nothingness. A collection of tombstones rose on a distant hill, the moonlight revealing their ghostly shapes.

Edward had been hired to replace Dr. Burrow, the recently deceased physician of Colfax County. Dr. Burrow, by all accounts, had been a young and energetic man with a taste for adventure. Colfax proved too wild for him. Searchers found the doctor's body at the bottom of a four-hundred-foot bluff after he had not returned from his morning hike. Edward never met Dr. Burrow but had overheard that he graduated first out of twenty-eight in his class. Edward, on the other hand, graduated eleventh out of thirteen students. He was not surprised to find himself somewhere rural and was content with the handsome salary the company was willing to pay. Colfax County desperately needed medical help and he wanted to be somewhere that he was useful. Dr. Burrow had been dead a month and since his passing all ailing and injured parties were forced to travel nearly forty miles for help. Although Edward was prepared to see his share of injury related to coal mining, he had very little experience with it in New York. Another of his concerns was keeping up with the rate at which the new town was reportedly growing.

Word of the riches hidden in the ground was drawing people of all backgrounds who wanted work.

"*Scusi*," came a voice that broke through Edward's thoughts, and he turned from the window. A young man boasting an exuberant hat and a red bandana knotted around his neck loomed over Edward's shoulder. His garb was excessive, but Edward held his tongue. "Are you a doctor?" the stranger asked with a thick accent, eyeing the medical book resting on the empty seat next to Edward.

"Yes," Edward answered. "I am the new doctor in Colfax. Are you acquainted with the town?"

"No," the man said. "This is the farthest west I've been. We come from *Italia*."

"We are from Campania," another man said, rising over the back of Edward's seat. This man had a more practical charm, wearing a clean suit and no hat. Other than their contrasting senses of style, the two men were nearly identical. Both were tall with similar dark eyes and distinctive wavy, brown hair.

"I have heard of Campania," said Edward, turning in his seat to face them. "You come for work?"

"We are wishing to work," the hatless man said. "We saw advertisement while staying in St. Louis. It has been hard for us to find any good work."

"It seems that you're in the right place," Edward said.

"I am Flavio Morreale and this is my little brother, Luca Morreale." Flavio flicked the brim of his brother's large hat in a playful manner that made Luca defensive.

"I am Dr. Edward Graf."

"Nice to meet you, Doctor," said Luca, holding his hand out. The two men had robust handshakes, giving Edward's knuckles a sharp pain with the pressure of each grip.

"Pleasure is mine," Edward said, noting with some surprise his own sincerity. The train began to slow. Steel screeched and protested under their feet, growing louder. Edward put his arm against the wall for support while Flavio and Luca stumbled forward, their weight pressing into the back of Edward's seat.

Luca leaned away and adjusted the red bandana around his neck. "Do you know where you'll be staying tonight, Doctor?" he asked.

"I believe my employer has accommodations for me at the clinic. And you?"

"Yes, we were told they had a place for us too. I wonder if our employer is the same. Are you working for the Colfax Coal Company?" Luca asked.

"Yes, that is my employer," Edward said. "The Colfax Coal Company and Mr. John Blair."

"Do you know Mr. Blair?" Luca inquired with interest.

"No, I haven't had the pleasure yet," Edward said. "He sent a letter to my mentor on behalf of his company. I was recommended and Mr. Blair accepted my credentials, but I have never personally spoken with him."

"He must be a great man," added Flavio. A whistle blew confirming the train's arrival. "Nice meeting you." Flavio nodded at his younger brother to collect his bags.

"Good luck to you both," Edward said, bidding them farewell. The view from the window had changed drastically since Edward's distraction from it. People were gathered outside; lights, horses, and motion swarmed about. He took his own bags out from the overhead storage and filed toward the exit. The streets of town were noisy with life. Thick clouds of dust swirled around brick-and-mortar buildings as townsfolk crossed every which way. When Edward made it to the clinic, he was taken aback by the enormity of it. The town's medical clinic was a great building. Steps led up to two large doors guarded by pillars on each side. Edward caught a feeling of panic in his chest as he stood at the foot of the entrance. He expected a small and unassuming place, not some grand hospital. Yet the building was dark and seemingly abandoned, while the town surrounding the facility clamored with life and leisure. People laughed, a horse trotted by pulling a wagon, and piano music echoed from some place farther down the lane. Edward stepped up to the entrance and knocked. It seemed a strange thing to do, but he was given no key and no instruction on what to do upon arrival.

"Anyone home?" came a voice from behind him.

"Oh, it doesn't seem so," Edward said, turning, embarrassed.

"You the new doctor?" the man asked. Edward squinted, unable to see the man through the glare of the streetlamp.

"I am. Dr. Edward Graf," he said.

"Ah, Graf," said the man. "Is that Swedish?"

"German, actually. And you are?"

"Llyod Dobbin." The man stepped forward into view and tilted his top hat in greeting. He was a smartly dressed man with a sarcastic grin. "I was the good Dr. Burrow's assistant, and I will continue to assist in what is needed."

"Mr. Dobbin, you are to be my friend, I believe."

"Only time will tell about that sort of thing." He gave Edward a look and approached, extending his hand.

"I hope I can live up to the late doctor's good reputation," Edward said, shaking the man's hand. Mr. Dobbin's grip was surprisingly warm and clammy for the autumn chill in the air.

"We'll have to wait and see," Mr. Dobbin answered. "Now, let's get you inside so you can see what you'll be working with."

"Much obliged for you meeting me at such an hour."

"I am an assistant, so I shall assist," he said as he unlocked the large front doors. Mr. Dobbin flipped a switch and the hall lit up before them. "I don't know if you're accustomed to this kind of electricity. The whole town is run off steam power created from the mines."

"From carbon monoxide," Edward said, mostly to himself.

"Exactly. I've found that it's prone to flicker most annoyingly," Mr. Dobbin said. "I'm sure you'll be able to see some of the coking ovens from your room upstairs. Do you want to see the facility tonight or wait until morning?"

"I think I'd like to peek my head in, just in case."

"I like the enthusiasm. Dr. Burrow was much the same, always ready to get to work. God rest his soul," Mr. Dobbin said, lowering his head in respect. "Well, over here is where most of the beds are held." He led Edward through a large room with roughly thirty beds.

"This facility holds thirty at a time?"

"It can hold more. We have more beds stored in the back and a spare room upstairs which can hold about five if needed, and the dining room could hold about ten beds in an emergency. That's just down the hall to the right."

"Good," said Edward. "It seems the town will need more than one doctor soon."

"Dr. Burrow often saw twenty patients at a time."

Fear struck Edward. He had never taken care of so many by himself all at once. He cleared his throat to expel the anxiety from his voice. "Sounds like I'll stay busy."

"Oh, you'll get used to it." Mr. Dobbin showed Edward through several areas of the facility, including the operating theatre and laboratory before guiding him to the kitchen and then his personal sleeping quarters. "You'll need your rest. I'm sure many will come in the morning. Some have been waiting to see a doctor since Dr. Burrow's death."

"Yes, I will rest now and see you in the morning," Edward said. "Thank you." Mr. Dobbin nodded and closed the door. It was a relatively small room with a fireplace, a small bed, a desk, and a little bookcase filled with medical books. Edward thumbed through the titles and was surprised to find many he didn't recognize: a pamphlet by Robert Koch titled "*Verfahren zur Untersuchung, zum Konservieren und Photographieren der Bakterien*" and other works by Ferdinand Cohn and August Carl Joseph Corda. Dr. Burrow was a man of stout learning—and Edward feared a far superior doctor than himself.

Edward undressed and climbed into his new bed, knowing sleep would not come easy his first night. He tried to push the thought of the recently deceased doctor from his mind, but he couldn't shake the realization that it wasn't long ago when Dr. Burrow himself had been living in the room, studying at the desk, and sleeping in the very bed Edward was resting in. He had large shoes to fill, and he hoped he wouldn't let the town down.

A loud pounding shook Edward from his rest. He quickly dressed and ran to the entrance of the clinic, the thunderous banging continuing all the while. "Yes, can I help you?" Edward called as he opened the door. He was met by the fist of a young woman, which nearly knocked him in the head. She gasped and stepped back. With her other arm, she was propping up a man. The man was hunched over, breathing heavily. "Come in!" Edward quickly showed them to a bed and began looking over the ill man.

"Tell me what happened?" he asked.

"My father just collapsed," the woman answered. "He was getting ready for work and fell. He said he is having trouble breathing. Do you think it's the coal miner's disease?"

Edward hesitated answering and found his stethoscope. He pressed the instrument to the man's chest and listened. Between the old man's wheezing, he heard the clinic door open and footsteps grow close behind him. "It's unlikely it has anything to do with coal dust," Edward said. "The mines here are equipped with the most modern ventilation systems and adhere to strict hygiene rules. It is doubtful that this is what some call coal workers' pneumoconiosis or coal workers' cough. Some recent studies even suggest that small amounts of coal dust are beneficial to the lungs."

"Dr. Graf, this may help." Edward turned to see Mr. Dobbin had entered the room with a steaming cup of tea.

"Tea?" Edward watched Mr. Dobbin with skepticism as he handed the tea to the patient. The old man gingerly sipped the cup, coughing violently with each swallow. "How did you know I had a patient?"

"My apartment is just beside the clinic. I hear most everything that happens at its door," answered Mr. Dobbin.

"My father has been coughing for months," the woman said. "Like so many of the men in town. Please, help him."

"There has been a bad batch of respiratory infection and consumption as of late, Dr. Graf."

The old man coughed again with such force that he buckled over from the violent need. Edward leaned him back and propped the pillows up behind him. "I don't think your father should go into work today," Edward said, looking over the old man's sinewy, thin form. "He needs to stay here until he feels better." The patient groaned but leaned back into the pillows.

"He works so hard and always feels ill," sighed the man's daughter. "With the opening of this new mine further south he has been called in too much."

"Stress can cause illness in even the strongest of men," Mr. Dobbin said.

"This is clearly more than stress," Edward said, giving Mr. Dobbin a glare.

"Of course," he answered. "I only meant stress can open the door to other illnesses."

"He's been acting strange lately." The woman was barely able to hide the quiver of her lips. "He keeps calling me by my mother's name. But…the other day he said he saw my mother in one of the shops. He ran after a poor, frightened stranger. He hasn't stopped talking about how he swore it was Mama and then other times he swears I am her. She's been buried in the cemetery for five years now."

"Rest will do him some good," Mr. Dobbin said.

"Mr. Dobbin, please make up some nice moist wash-cloths to help him rest. I'll give him a little diamorphine to aid in his cough and stay up with him until he sleeps. You are welcome to stay," Edward said, turning to the woman. "What's your name?"

"Gloria Peirez. This is my father, Anselmo."

The night lingered on and Mr. Dobbin left for his apartment. Edward nodded off in his seat at the desk across the room, occasionally jolted awake again by a violent coughing fit from Mr. Peirez. Edward tried his best to comfort the old man and his daughter and eventually the clinic was silent, and all rested peacefully. The morning hours brought other patients, most with minor issues. When the hour had nearly reached noon, Edward went to wake Mr. Peirez but found that he would not wake. He felt no pulse. The man was cool to the touch. It was clear that the old man had been dead for nearly an hour. Edward looked over to Gloria, who had suddenly risen. "He's gone. Isn't he?"

Edward nodded. "I'm sorry."

Edward's heart grew heavy; his nerves were jolted by the death of his first patient. Mr. Peirez was gone, but Edward knew he was the first of many who would die while under his care at the Colfax County clinic. Cemeteries in towns rich in mineral deposits always had a way of growing, and as the weeks passed, Edward saw case after case of men with bothersome coughs filter in through the doors of the clinic. Many were easily treated by reducing their tobacco use, but a few of the older men had more severe bronchitis.

The attitudes of the town seemed to turn along with the season. Colfax became a refuge of warmth as winter grew near and the desert turned more bitter with every passing day. Yet being confined indoors only reminded Edward of Gloria Peirez's words from that first night. "My father has been coughing…like so many of the men in town." Edward could not ignore the persistence with which every coal miner in town had some form of bronchitis or pneumonia or pesky tickle in their throat.

Between patients Edward plunged into the books that the late Dr. Burrow left behind. Some raised interesting questions on disease in coal miners. However, they contradicted the other works Edward had read at school. Edward's instructors had asserted small amounts of coal dust strengthened the lungs, while Dr. Burrow's books questioned that conclusion. It was truly strange, uncanny even, how little the women in town coughed compared to the coal miners. Edward was considering all this in his study when he felt it.

The clinic shook and thunder rumbled underfoot. Edward ran to the window to see smoke billowing just beyond the south side of town. He quickly dressed and grabbed medical supplies.

"It's the new mine," Mr. Dobbin said as he met Edward outside the hospital. The streets were filled with townspeople. Panicked voices and yells rang out through the avenues. Many ran in the direction of the mine.

"Have Sheriff Carter collect volunteers to help bring men out!" Edward yelled, sprinting by Mr. Dobbin. He was shocked to see many residents had already arrived and were crowded outside the cloudy entrance of the mine. Many were holding back sobbing women and children as they tried to enter the mine after loved ones, while others were already starting rescue efforts. Soon bodies began appearing from the smokey mouth of the mine. Edward ran to all those pulled from rubble. Most were already dead.

"Doctor, this one's alive!" a voice called out. Edward ran toward the voice.

A thick layer of coal dust clung to the body and Edward searched for injury. He realized who the man was. "Flavio," Edward gasped. He pulled back Flavio's tattered clothing and looked over his face and head. "You're okay, friend. Little more than a few cuts and nicks."

"Luca is gone," Flavio rasped, coughing. "I know my brother is gone. Right before it collapsed, I saw Luca. He was eaten up by the dust."

Just then, Edward saw Mr. Dobbin, Sheriff Carter, and a few men approach—their faces stoic and focused. "I need him taken to the clinic," Edward said to the men.

Edward continued to find only the dead as the bodies were exhumed. Flavio's brother, Luca, was the last corpse to be pulled from the rubble. By then night had fallen and the young man's injuries made him unrecognizable. No trace of his warm smile remained. None of the cheer or optimism that Edward had found so endearing. Edward was only able to assert that the body was Luca's from the red bandana tied around his neck.

"What do you suppose made the foreman do it?" Mr. Dobbin asked later that evening, inquiring a little louder than Edward wished. Edward saw Flavio perk up from his hospital bed across the room. Twenty-six men had perished in the incident caused by the cave-in. Rumors were stirring up like the cold desert dust about a deranged foreman and a deliberate action.

"He kept repeating, 'We have to keep them from getting out. We have to trap them,'" Flavio said. His voice was weak.

Mr. Dobbin gulped. "Heavens."

Edward went toward Flavio's bed, moving closer to ask him a question. "What do you suppose he was talking about, Flavio?"

"U-Umbria."

"Umbria? What is that?"

"It is…a myth…where I came from," Flavio said. "She is the goddess of darkness and secrets."

"What on earth is he going on about, Edward?" said Mr. Dobbin.

Flavio continued his voice growing cold, "Sometimes the men see things in the shadows. Dark things."

"Have you seen anything?" Edward asked. "Flavio?"

But the young man leaned back again and closed his eyes for sleep.

"Poor thing," Edward said, "what a horrible day to endure." Edward leaned down and pulled the blankets up over Flavio's shoulders to keep him warm before heading to his room.

Edward lay in bed with the lamp extinguished but couldn't fight the visions of the bodies, blackened by fire and coal dust. He had washed the dust from his face and arms but was too tired to scrub all the black soot from his skin. The smell of coal rock lingered in his nose as he lay. It was a smokey, caustic smell. He tossed and turned, unable to find relief. He gave in, got out of bed, and lit a fire in his hearth. Not wanting to wake anyone to draw him a bath, he took the booklet from Dr. Borrow's collection, *Verfahren zur*

Untersuchung, zum Konservieren und Photographieren der Bakterien by Robert Koch. He opened the pamphlet and an envelope tumbled out onto the floor. Edward bent down and picked it up. It was addressed to Dr. R. Koch Kreisphysikus in Wollstein, Germany. Edward peeled the envelope open— empty. Whatever Dr. Burrow had planned on sending the author had been lost along with him. Edward took a seat and began to thumb through the booklet. It showed photographs of bacteria. He tried to recall what little German he had learned in his youth. He knew of the physician Robert Koch, but many of his mentors believed his work was not worth studying in detail. Edward couldn't help but delve deeper into the document. "*B. anthracis*," Edward mumbled, searching the pages for understanding. "*Glasruthsche*…glass slide." He searched his memory for translation. "Dry fix bacterial culture slide. Determine causative agent." He was transfixed for what must have been hours, only to be pulled away by a sudden groan outside his window. Edward stood and peered outside. Down below, he saw a man, stumbling and moaning near the back door. "I'll kill ya! I'll kill anyone who tries to touch me!" the man said.

Edward quickly searched for a weapon, finding only the antique pistol which he had received as a graduation present. He wanted to help the man, if he could, and protect himself if he must. He was not even sure the thing could still fire. He walked down the stairs. The hall was silent but for the muffled growls of the man outside. Edward hurried down the hall and checked the patients' beds. A young woman who had been resting at her husband's bedside looked up and approached. "Doctor, is everything okay?" The loose bun on top of her head moved as she walked and stray, dark ringlets fell around her face.

"Could you run and lock the front? If you can, miss," he said.

"What's wrong?" she asked.

"There's a disturbed man loitering at the back door. Can't you hear him?"

"No," she gasped. "My thoughts have been elsewhere. I will go lock it." The woman ran down the hall toward the entrance.

Edward grabbed some rope from the operating theatre and ran to the back door. Anxiety overwhelmed Edward's emotions. He never fared well in physically violent situations. He had not had good success in de-escalating a violent patient's anger. With shaking hands, he checked that the latch was in place. He held his breath and leaned into the door to listen. The man's growls grew louder. "It's poisoned! But I'll kill them first," the man slurred and spat just on the other side of the door. "Oh, the shakes," he gurgled. "So thirsty, but it's poisoned. Makes me sick to swallow even my own words."

Edward sprang away. He had heard the complaint once before from a man who had contracted rabies from a mad dog in New York. It was a horrible situation that Edward had only recently put from his mind. Now, he might have another hopeless case. He unlocked the latch and gripped the door-knob, preparing to make his move. The growls and profanity from the man were growing more violent. Edward whispered a countdown from three and then burst through the door. He looked around, ready to subdue the man, but the area was silent. The man was gone. Edward quickly searched the alley behind the hospital. "I'm a doctor!" Edward yelled. "I can help." The street remained silent and there was no sign of the man.

"Dr. Graf," called the woman from inside the clinic.

"Yes," he answered, hurrying toward her. Her hair had completely fallen from its bun and now rested in a mess around her shoulders.

"There's a family here with an old woman who claims to have been mauled by a bear." Edward followed the woman through the door. Glancing at the alley one last time before locking the back door tight.

Edward approached two men and a horror-stricken old woman. "Our mother claims a bear attacked her near her house," one of the men said.

Edward asked her sons to help hold her arms down as she thrashed and cried. He looked over her body. "There's not a scratch on her," Edward said.

The men looked at him, baffled. Both men were weary and covered in dust, evidently not yet having a chance to wash after the day's tragic events.

"Ma'am," Edward began, "where did the beast make contact?"

"Oh, my face! My stomach. Everywhere!" she yelled. The other patients began to stir in their beds and Edward quickly inspected her again. "Just like when it got my brother. Oh, that beast shredded George to bits."

"I see no evidence of an animal attack. I see no bite or scratch of any kind. Where is your brother now?"

"Our Uncle George died long ago," the older son answered.

"That's Mrs. Rossi," Flavio said. He staggered from his bed and stood next to Edward.

Edward noted the name. "Lorenzo Rossi?" he asked.

"Yes," the younger son said. "Our father died in the explosion today. She was outside the mine all day waiting for his body, and when he was found it took hours to separate them." There were dry streaks staining the man's face where tears had cut through grime.

It was clear to Edward that the woman was having a bout of hysteria, so he had her sons escort her up to a private room and mixed up a sleeping draft for her to take. The woman's sobs grew faint as she was guided away.

"Poor Mrs. Rossi," said Flavio, returning to his bed to curl up as though he were a child fearful of nightmares.

"Would you also like me to make you a sleeping draft?"

"Yes, please, Doctor. Just this once," he answered.

After things in the clinic had settled, Edward sent word to the sheriff that there may be a dangerous man on the loose. One that Edward believed may have contracted rabies. But the man was not found, and no other reports were made.

A mass funeral was held for the twenty-six men who lost their lives in the South #4 Mine. Monuments to the dead spread like white capped mushrooms across the once bare desert. It took several weeks until the mine was reopened. Edward's stomach rolled at the thought of Flavio reentering the very place he saw his brother perish. A month went by before Edward saw Flavio again. When he did return to the hospital it was to speak to Edward in private.

"I have avoided coming here Doctor," said Flavio, seated at the dining room table. Edward filled him a glass of whiskey and took a seat next to him.

"You don't need to feel hesitant about seeking care, not for any reason," Edward said.

"It is only that I am unsure that my problem is a medical concern." Flavio took a tentative sip from his glass.

"Well, as your friend, whatever it is, I will try and help."

"For over three weeks now, there have been sightings of a man in the South #4 Mine."

"Who is this man?" Edward's thoughts rushed back to the man at the back door. But he knew if the man had been viral, he would have perished long ago.

"It is Luca."

"Luca," Edward said. "What do you mean?"

"At first, I thought I was going mad and did not tell a soul when I would see him. But I kept seeing him, and with Luca being so popular with the others and always joking with us, I decided to tell a few others and they soon began seeing him in the same area I had before. I am certain it is him."

"Have they seen him in town?"

"No," Flavio answered. "Only in the mine. He used to stay hidden. Always sticking to newly blasted areas and the most remote parts of the mine. But he is beginning to go to other areas. I see him almost every day now."

"Who else says they've seen him?" Edward asked.

"Ask anyone who works in South #4," Flavio said. "Most have seen him."

Edward sat back in his chair. "But you saw Luca buried. I saw his body and pronounced him dead myself."

"I am convinced it wasn't him."

"You believe it was someone else's body?"

"Yes," said Flavio. "You said yourself that the face was very badly mangled, and you only decided it was Luca because of his red bandana."

"That is true," said Edward. "But then why was Luca not found among the survivors?"

"I don't know why he would hide."

"Has he spoken to you when you see him?"

"*Mors vincit omnia.*"

"What?"

"Death conquers all. He has only said this. I believe he's gone mad, Doctor."

A town meeting was held to address Flavio's testimony. Over fifteen men had reported seeing Luca in the South #4 Mine. Edward along with Sheriff Carter were asked to exhume Luca's coffin and inspect the contents for further evidence. Flavio supplied Edward with family pictures which would aid in the identification. The miners were set to search South #4 the following morning, volunteering their time.

"The whole town has gone nutty," Sheriff Carter said as his deputies lifted Luca's coffin from the ground. Dirt swirled and drifted with the wind in the glare of the setting sun.

"It'll be dark soon," Edward said. "May I borrow your lantern for better light?" The sheriff handed Edward his lantern and the men pried open the coffin. A putrid smell overcame Edward, but he forced his gaze forward, not wanting any ill repute from the sheriff or deputies for being a doctor with a weak stomach for death.

The dry climate and cold had aided well in the preservation of the body, yet it had not stopped decomposition. Edward could not tell whether the dark substance surrounding the body was decay or coal dust. He reached into the coffin and unwrapped the red bandana from the neck. Edward coughed out the revolting smell of death and coal dust. He tried to refrain from vomiting.

"Well, is it Luca Morreale?" asked Sheriff Carter.

Edward carefully examined the family photos provided by Flavio. They were the only pictures Flavio had of his brother. In one photograph he and his brother could not have been older than seven. The black and white image crackled along the edges of the photo, yet the boy's faces and forms were clear and detailed. They were each holding a flag and smiling under a tree. Their parents must have been proud to have had such healthy progeny. Edward moved to the next photo. It must have been taken shortly before their arrival in Colfax County. Luca had on the same ridiculous hat he was wearing the night Edward met him on the train. Edward searched the photos, holding the lantern close to the images in the dying light.

"Luca has a darkening on his right hand just above the thumb in both these photos. Perhaps a birthmark."

The sheriff leaned close to inspect the photographs. "I see it," he agreed.

Edward took the dead body's stiff right hand in his own as Sheriff Carter held the lantern up for a better look. He spat into the dead man's bandana and scrubbed the hand, removing the stains of dark dust. "There's the mark," Edward said, with a hint of sadness. "This must be the body of Luca Morreale."

Edward watched as the deputies hammered fresh nails into the coffin and lowered it back down into the ground.

"You ready, Doctor?" asked Sheriff Carter.

"It's not quite dark," Edward said. "I think I'll walk back to town."

"Keep the lantern, just in case. And be aware, there's been a lot of bear sightings lately."

"Thank you, Sheriff." Edward listened to the wagon move away, until it was little more than a whisper on the wind. Silence collected and the night gave off a sense of eerie solitude. Edward couldn't help but feel saddened by his confirmation. He had allowed himself, like the others, to hope that Luca had not perished with the other men that day. He looked across the expanse of tombstones. He had known many of the souls buried in the ground before him.

"*Mors vincit omnia*," he whispered to the growing darkness. The thought sent a chill down his spine and he turned to head home. With a start, he noticed a figure in the distance.

"Hello, there," Edward called to the person. The figure's lantern glistened through the growing darkness and Edward looked at his own lantern, its light weakening from low fuel. "Excuse me, do you mind if I join you? My light seems to be dying." The figure turned and started down the road. "Excuse me, wait!"

Edward rushed after the figure. Something deep inside him needed to see who it was. The person began to pick up speed as Edward followed. "Wait, I'm not going to hurt you. I just wish to share your lamplight." Edward soon realized he was running to catch the person, and as he gained ground, he saw that it was a man with the same gait and height as Flavio. "Flavio, wait! I need to speak with you!"

Flavio continued down the road, Edward lagging until they reached the mouth of the South #4 Mine. Flavio stopped. Edward held his lantern up high to illuminate the ground better as he approached his friend.

"Why did you run?" Edward asked, placing a hand on the man's back. The man turned to greet him, and Edward fell backward to the ground. "Luca…it…it can't be." Edward's sight was clouded with fear and then everything turned to darkness.

He woke in the clinic, his throat dry and scratchy.

"Why on earth were you at the mouth of a mine, Edward?" asked Mr. Dobbin.

"Who found me?" Edward moaned, sitting up.

"Sheriff Carter brought you in. They went back to the cemetery to find you after you didn't return, and they followed your trail to the mine."

"Did they see just my footprints?"

"They didn't mention any others. Why?"

"Nothing," said Edward. Mr. Dobbin gave him a suspicious stare. "What time is it?"

"It's nearly six a.m.," answered Mr. Dobbin. "Men are lining up for work at the mines by now. Thank God, Sheriff Carter found you before they did. That's the last thing this town needs. Their doctor fainting everywhere."

"There will be no search party?" Edward asked.

"Of course not," said Mr. Dobbin. "You proved that Luca Morreale was in that coffin last night. The men must be playing some sort of joke."

Edward looked at his hands. The grooves and lines of his palms still covered in the grime of last night's work. "I need to go into that mine."

"What? Why?"

Edward leaped from his bed, ignoring Mr. Dobbin. He quickly took a book from Dr. Borrow's library and ran to the laboratory for supplies.

The morning sun warmed Edward's face as he made his way toward the South #4 Mine. He saw the coal miners making their way through the mouth of the mine, disappearing into the cold darkness within.

"Doctor?" Flavio appeared from the mass of workers. "Doctor have you decided to restart the search?"

"I can't say at the moment," Edward answered. "I need in the mine."

"I…I am not allowed to bring you," said Flavio. "The foreman may accompany you in…my boss. I'll take you to him. But, I must ask, is it true? Was it Luca?"

"It was your brother in that coffin. I'm sorry."

"But…how?" Flavio gasped, placing a hand to his brow. "We have all seen him."

Edward handed Flavio the family photographs he had allowed him to borrow and moved toward the mouth of the mine. Flavio stayed behind as Edward weaved through the men toward the entrance.

"Hey, you! Stop right there!" a voice yelled. "Doctor Graf, you should not go in there unaccompanied."

Edward grabbed a safety lamp and hurried into the entrance. The sound of rock hammering boomed through the dark cavern. The smell of coal was overwhelming. Edward's nostrils burned with the unfamiliar strength of the scent. He continued mostly unnoticed by the men who were concentrating on breaking and loading coal into the cars. As he walked deeper in, fewer men were around, and the sounds of work became soft and distant. Edward turned off the main tunnel and probed deeper under the earth. The black ceiling above grew close and oppressive. Edward was alone. His breath grew heavy in the emptiness and he held his lantern up high. The long narrow passage seemed to go on endlessly. He searched the walls for a clue, a sign of anything odd as he made his way down the tunnel, occasionally squatting down to pass through. Mysterious echoes took the place of human noise. Pungent scents began to attach themselves to Edward's nostrils. He approached a wall and searched its inky surface. Edward began to hear coughing somewhere off in the darkness and followed it. The coughing grew louder and the number of men suffering from the affliction seemed to be increasing as well.

"Hello?" Edward asked the darkness. "It's Dr. Graf." Edward's boots began slipping out from under him as loose coal gravel shifted underfoot. Faces and stumbling forms appeared in the view of his lamplight. Deformed, crushed, and wheezing. Men walked straight toward Edward. Edward closed his eyes and held his hands to his ears, trying to force them away, but the sight of the walking dead was replaced only by the clawing of fingernails. "No!" he yelled. "You can't be real!" He scrambled away from the clutching forms.

Edward struggled to focus as the ailing men pulled and tugged at his clothes. He lurched away from their grasping arms and found the wall, flattening his body against it. He faced the rock and breathed in the thick scent of subterranean earth. Fumbling for a test tube in his satchel, Edward took a scraping from the wall, his hands trembling in terror. He fought his way through the coughing, soot-covered men and took out a new test tube and scraped another sample. He took an uneven breath and placed the tubes safely in his bag.

"Please, leave me alone!" he cried out as the gruesome men continued to surround him. Edward struggled to remember his way out. The tunnel became unfamiliar to him as he tried to escape the horrors around him. The rock walls slithered. Something flickered orange and red beyond. A hot gale struck at Edward's face, pulling tears from his eyes. "No!" he gasped as a wall of flame edged toward him.

"There he is!" a man yelled. "Dr. Graf, what do you think you're doing? It's dangerous back here alone."

"The fire!" Edward yelled. "Run, you fool!"

A pleasant smell of sandalwood wafted through Mr. John Blair's office. Edward sat stiffly in a chair, awaiting the arrival of the owner of Colfax County Coal. The door swung open, releasing the scent of cigar smoke and strong cologne.

"Dr. Graf, is it?" Mr. Blair said. He wore a narrow lapel and silk shirt with four golden buttons. He puffed smoke from a large cigar between his teeth. "I am sorry it has taken me so long to meet you in person. I hear nothing but good things…excluding some of the more recent events near the South #4 Mine."

"Yes, sir. That is why I am here," Edward began. "I would like to address a problem with the mine and possibly others. It is my belief that the South #4 Mine needs to be shut down immediately."

Mr. Blair's eyebrows rose in surprise. "Now why would I want to shut down the best producing mine in the area?"

"Mr. Blair, sir," Edward continued, "I have written up here in my hands proof that there is a bacterium releasing spores in that mine. Upon testing the samples, I found that it altered the behavior of animal subjects drastically. And it is my belief that exposure to this germ has produced strong hallucinations in town and in the mines. Anyone who comes in contact with the spore in the coal dust is susceptible. Perhaps one such hallucination even resulted in the death of the twenty-six miners in the South #4 Mine earlier this year."

"The crazy foreman who caused the cave-in?"

"Yes."

"That sounds quite serious. And you have experienced these hallucinations, is that correct?"

"I did. I believe the effects can vary from person to person."

"But you have probably been exposed to these…spores. So, what have you seen? I mean, I was told of your behavior in the mine. You were screaming of fire and death, yet there was nothing but coal."

"Yes," answered Edward. "I have been exposed and witnessed the effects of exposure to the germ. However, ending the exposure and taking in fresh untainted air will stop all hallucinations."

"How can you be sure, Doctor?"

"I suppose, I can't. Not yet. But I have witnessed behavior returning to normal in patients and in my animal subjects. I also stopped hallucinating shortly after I escaped the dust and bathed. Exposure to the germ has not impeded my scientific investigation, if that's what you're inferring."

"What do these germs look like?"

"The spores are microscopic. I have samples of them in the clinic laboratory. They are elongated. Able to live in the dirt and coal. I believe they spread through dust once disturbed."

"Well, it sounds a bit fanciful. Little creatures living in the dust. There has been an awful lot of woe and stress of late. Especially for you, Doctor. I've been thinking we need something to occupy our minds, perhaps a festival."

"Mr. Blair, the people in this town are in danger," Edward said, aghast. "They need to stay out of the mines until we can run more tests and figure out a way to stop the spores from infecting. There could be long-term physiological effects from prolonged exposure or another bad incident. We need to stop the shipment of all coal from the South #4 Mine until further notice and test all the coal going out for the bacteria. It could impact anyone who comes in contact with the coal. We don't know how someone could react. They could react violently. They could die."

Mr. Blair's cigar went limp between his lips. He collected it with his fingers and set it in an ashtray on his desk. "Can anyone test for these spores like you have?"

"With modern medicine it is very possible, but someone would have to suspect the coal, and many things are often lost in a confusion of other possibilities, very much like coal miners' cough."

"Coal miners' cough?" Mr. Blair slowly rounded his desk and leaned against the corner nearest to Edward. Edward knew he had made a mistake. "There's no such thing as coal miners' cough. All our doctors say so. Do you have anything published on these spores you've discovered?"

Edward gulped. "I only have what I brought with me." He had samples at the clinic, but all written evidence he now held in his hands.

Mr. Blair took the papers from Edward and set them on his desk. "Sheriff Carter!" Mr. Blair called. The sheriff entered through the door and stood at Edward's side. "Carter, I think the two of us need to accompany Dr. Graf into South #4." He looked back to Edward, taking his cigar and sucking a final drag before extinguishing it. "I want to see where you think these things live."

"Let's go, then," Sheriff Carter said. His large hands clawed into the tops of Edward's shoulders and began escorting him from the room. Mr. Blair followed.

A two-horse buggy sat outside Mr. Blair's office. "Go ahead and sit up front with Mr. Blair, Doctor. I'll take the back," the sheriff said. Edward climbed in, taking an anxious gulp as he followed orders. The sudden forced change of scenery made him uneasy. Mr. Blair sat next to him, holding the reins in his gloved hands. The horses began to walk. They went slowly, and Mr. Blair waved at all those who stopped to look. Edward examined his employer. Mr. John Blair's benevolent smile and rich look were things he both envied and hated.

"You won't be able to see the germs with your eyes. We'd have to go back to the clinic for that," Edward said.

"I just want to see the place where you found these things, for now," Mr. Blair said, waving and smiling at a woman as they drove by. "Then we can move forward."

"I'll need to collect samples from other parts of the mine too," Edward said. "We can't be sure it's only this one area."

"You're right," Mr. Blair said, nodding. The buggy continued toward the mine. The air was cool and crisp, but the sun warmed Edward. They slowed to a stop near the mouth of the mine and Mr. Blair jumped out, patting one of the horses on its shoulder. Few men were outside, most were busy with work inside the mine.

A foreman approached as the three men neared the entrance. "Mr. Blair, we weren't expecting you," the man said.

"Sheriff Carter, Dr. Graf, and I just want to have a look around," he said.

"Is the doctor well enough?" he asked.

Mr. Blair laughed, slapping Edward on the back. "Are you feeling better after your last experience in the mine, Doctor?"

Edward lurched forward from the force of the slap. "I'm feeling quite well," Edward answered. He straightened his jacket, smoothing out the wrinkles Mr. Blair caused with the force of his blow.

"Well, I will follow you in," the foreman said.

"No need," Mr. Blair said. "We know where we're going. Don't we, Dr. Graf?"

"Yes," Edward said, his stomach in knots at Mr. Blair's commanding tone. The foreman looked concerned but held his tongue at Mr. Blair's behest.

"After you, Dr. Graf," Mr. Blair said. Edward walked forward. The sun left them as they entered the mine. They each took a safety lamp and carried them as they walked by the men working. Many stopped to notice Mr. Blair. He took a moment to greet them with a smile and good word before continuing behind Edward.

The walls grew tighter as they went further into the mine. They turned off in the direction Edward remembered from last time. He noticed a few changes in the walls as they walked. Workers had been chipping away at a seam along the wall but were no longer around. The three were alone. The noises of the workers grew faint and the only lights to guide them were their own lamps. Mr. Blair took a handkerchief from his pocket and held it to his face. Edward paused a moment and decided to do the same. He searched his pockets and found his own handkerchief, then placed it over his nose and mouth with one hand. Sheriff Carter shook his head at the unmanly action. Edward doubted the man had ever owned anything as genteel as a handkerchief.

Edward's chest grew tight as they crept farther back into darkness. He held the handkerchief firm to his face as he searched the dark corners and hidden places of the underground labyrinth.

Soon the world turned utterly quiet. The walls grew close and Edward bent down to pass a low spot. Only the breath of the three men and the gravel shifting under their feet reached Edward's ears.

"Are we near the place yet?" Mr. Blair asked. "Haven't seen anyone for a while."

"Almost," Edward said.

"I don't know, boss," Sheriff Carter grunted. "Those workers aren't too far away."

"Too far away for what?" Edward asked, stopping.

"A little farther back and it'll be fine," Mr. Blair replied.

"Keep going and show us the place, Dr. Graf," Sheriff Carter said, nudging him along.

The hair on the back of Edward's neck began to stand on end. Something wasn't right. Their remoteness and his escorts' persistence sent an alarm through his body. He stopped again. "Why shouldn't we have the foreman join us?" Edward asked. "He should find out where the spores are. Then he could tell the men what areas to avoid."

"Go on. He'll know soon enough," Sheriff Carter said.

Edward turned back toward the darkness. The scent of coal filled the air. He continued a few moments before recognizing the place. Holding the handkerchief firmly to his face, he said in a muffled voice, "I took samples from that wall and this one."

Edward squinted, trying to make out the two men with him. Their lanterns flickered softly in the darkness. Sheriff Carter's illuminated figure stood in stark relief against absolute darkness. The sheriff glanced back toward the way out and then turned his attention to Edward. "Very good," Mr. Blair said, approaching Edward. "Show us exactly where they are."

Edward looked at Sheriff Carter, noticing something large and round in his hand. "What's the point of that? I can't recall the exact place I took the scrapings. I found them here though."

"Turn around," Sheriff Carter said.

Edward shifted on his feet, making out the item in Sheriff Carter's hand. It was a large rock. "What's happening here?" he asked.

"What do you mean?" Mr. Blair asked, still holding the handkerchief to his face. "You're showing us where to find these things."

"That's not really why you brought me here, is it?"

Mr. Blair shook his head and said, "You doctors are always testing my patience." Edward stepped back, finding himself against a wall. "I really thought you would work better for us. What was the other one's name?"

"Dr. Burrow," Sheriff Carter answered.

"Yes, well, he burrowed himself into an early grave, didn't he?" Mr. Blair said. "This one wasn't supposed to be as meticulous. I thought he was last in his class or something."

Edward held the handkerchief over his mouth, now covering panicked gasps.

"Do it quickly. Quietly," Mr. Blair said. "We can say something fell on his head."

"Everyone knows you're with me!" Edward said.

Edward's heart raced. Sheriff Carter set his lantern down. The sheriff loomed over Edward, dark and large. Edward held his lamp out as if to ward off evil. He opened his mouth to scream for help, but a cry from Sheriff Carter split the darkness instead. He dropped the rock and started frantically wiping at his arms. "Get them off!" the sheriff yelled. "Oh, help me! Get them off me!"

Edward bolted away from the man and his hallucination, but Mr. Blair caught Edward's jacket and pulled him down to the ground. Edward's lantern went flying, hitting Sheriff Carter. The man tore at the lamp as if it were an animal attacking, damaging the protective wire gauze surrounding the flame. Sheriff Carter let out a yell as flames spread across his body. The sheriff ran, hitting a wall, and sank to the ground in shrieking anguish. The screams from the sheriff echoed back from distant parts of the cavern. Edward and Mr. Blair rolled and twisted around in a struggle to get up.

Mr. Blair made it to his feet first and kicked Edward. Edward grabbed his leg, forcing Mr. Blair to fall back to the ground. They traded punches, rolling and scraping across the ground, and then Mr. Blair bellowed in pain and surprise. The man's pant leg was a flaming, kicking torch. Instinct compelled Edward to spring toward Mr. Blair's leg, ready to beat the flame with his bare hands, but he was met by swinging fists. "The secret dies with you!" Mr. Blair spat in his rage, trying to pull Edward into the flames spreading over his leg.

Edward broke free. "Fire!" he yelled. He turned, bolting down the dark tunnel, hands stinging from the friction as he tried to guide himself blindly. He found the intersection of shafts and turned right, swiftly feeling his way through the mine. After a few terror-stricken moments, he reached a group of men who had heard the commotion. Edward grabbed onto one of them. "Fire…Sheriff Carter…Mr. Blair."

"Fire!" the man said, eyes growing wide. "There's firedamp back there! Run!" he yelled, turning to rush away. Edward followed. The alarm sounded and men ran to escape. The world shook, pushing Edward to the ground. He anticipated debris, suffocation, and heat, but it never came. Edward saw firemen in soaked wool go by, heading toward the back, but they were too late to save the two men.

After the horrible events of the day, Edward sat at his desk. He had washed the dust from his hair and body and now sipped whiskey to calm his nerves. He took a pen in his hand and put it to paper. He would start with his findings on the bacteria, and he would demand the permanent closure of the South #4 Mine. Edward's fists tightened. He could trust none of the other town officials, deputies, or whoever replaced the sheriff. Was Mr. Dobbin even an ally? The conspiring forces had already succeeded in silencing him once, but regardless of whether they'd be successful the next time, word of the bacteria and its danger must escape town. There was one person he trusted, who had given his life pursuing the truth. Edward set his pen down and picked up Dr. Koch's pamphlet and found the envelope addressed to the author. Dr. Burrow had planned to send Koch a letter. Edward would send one instead.

THE
ENUMERATOR

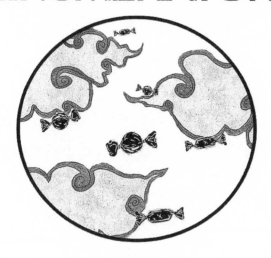

The work of a census enumerator is grueling and exacting. One needs the utmost stamina and good will toward his fellow citizen to undertake such an immense task. Horus was such a man—a loyal and confident patriot. The month of April in rural Kansas was mild most years. This particular April was a kind 68 degrees and Horus needed little more than a light jacket to get through his day. He found the small town of Fredonia, Kansas, pleasant and quiet. As per the last record, 3,446 people resided in the Wilson County seat. It was a pleasant hillock town known for its cement and soybeans. Horus stepped out of his room at the Gold Dust Hotel, sipping his morning joe. He took a seat on the front porch of the hotel and examined the town.

There was little activity in the town square in the early hours. The sidewalks and storefronts were tidy. The main road made a box around the Wilson County Courthouse and park. Horus watched birds wash in a nearby puddle and drank his coffee. The door to the front of the hotel creaked open and John Hunter, Horus's manager, stepped out, carrying his own steaming cup of coffee.

"Morning, Horus." John tipped his hat in greeting. "Is that the new Chevrolet with sealed beam headlights?"

Horus looked over at his car. The car's silver grill and glossy black paint shimmered in the morning light. "Yup," Horus said, "I got a pretty deal on it."

"I might put you on the rural east side since you've got such nice headlights. Farmers can be hard to track down. You might not be back until nightfall."

"I don't mind," said Horus. "Are the others up?"

"Most headed over there for breakfast." John pointed across the square at a cafe.

"Well, I've eaten," Horus said, rising from his seat. "So, I guess I'll be on my way."

"Do you have everything you need?"

"Yes, sir," Horus said. "You supplied us with everything we needed yesterday."

"You've got a total of 31 houses. We will meet up at about 8 p.m. Sound good?" John handed Horus a list of addresses.

"Yes, sir," Horus said, setting down his coffee to inspect the list. "I will do my best to get everyone." Horus took a final sip of coffee and headed toward his car. The heavy door squeaked open and he took a seat on the leather upholstery. He set his list down, checked that he had enough candies to give the children that may inhabit each home, and he began his journey.

Horus took in the colors of spring. The blues and greens were something both peculiar and lovely to him. His car was slow, yet deliberate. He knew he had to have patience to finish his task for the day, and as he pulled up to his first house, he was greeted by a young woman hanging clothes on a line.

"Hello, ma'am," Horus said, exiting his car. He tipped his hat to the woman and smiled.

"Hello," she answered. "Can I help you?"

"I am with the United States Census Bureau. Can you spare a few moments to fill out the 1940 census for our records?"

"Oh, yes," she said. "We were told you were coming today. Let me go get Dean." The woman headed toward the house and Horus followed behind. As he approached the porch, he spotted two small children. Their mother popped inside the front door and Horus greeted the children. "Hello, kids. Would you like some candy?" he asked, pulling the treats from his pocket. The children took them happily without question.

"Thank you," one said.

"Thanks, sir," said the other.

"Of course," he said. "It isn't every day that someone from the census comes to your door, you know."

"Oh, thank you," their mom said as she reemerged from the door. "Kids, what do you say?"

"Oh, they had perfect manners," Horus said. "They both already said thank you. Are there only two children? Did I miss giving anyone candy?"

"Oh, no. We only have two at the moment," said the woman.

The children smiled as they stuck the sweet treats into their mouths. "I hope you enjoy," Horus said.

"Here's my husband," the woman said as a man opened the door to welcome Horus.

"Hello, sir, do you mind taking a few moments to fill out the census?"

"Of course not," answered the man, happily taking the sheet and pen from Horus. Horus's day of enumerating went by like clockwork, as many people were aware that men from the census would be making rounds that day. At each stop, Horus prided himself on his manners and gave each child a piece of candy. As 8 p.m. approached, Horus began to make his way back to town. The country road was getting dark. He turned his headlights on and looked up. A green ball of light lit up the sky above him and Horus slowed. The light grew brighter and fiercer. He pulled his car over to the side of the road. "Right on time," he said, taking his packet and opening the door to step out of the car.

A warm wind greeted him as he stood from the car and a green beam of light engulfed him, lifting his body from the road. He soon found himself inside a ship. Its chrome interior shone like a million fine diamonds. Horus dusted himself off and organized his papers neatly.

"Did you do what we needed?" John asked, approaching him from the helm.

"Yes, sir," Horus answered. "All the children I saw today happily took the candy. Here is the list of those I infected." Horus handed John his packet. "Have the others finished their missions?"

"Yes, you are the last one."

"When will we be ready?"

"Not yet. This world is about to be at war and my supervisor says we should wait at least 81 Earth years. Their species should be greatly weakened by that time and there will be another census that year. The sensors we gave the children will help us monitor and understand their biology better. He should know when we return if it's safe to take over."

"Looking forward to helping out in any way I can," Horus said, smiling.

TECH
TORRENT

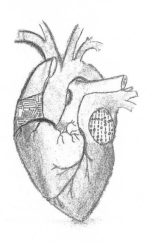

Calla turned over on her side. Chill air touched her neck, and she moved her blanket over her head to hide in the warmth and darkness of the comforter. Her small apartment was always cold in the morning. Her heat kicked off around 4 a.m. and the cold seeped in through the thin, uninsulated walls. She called awake the small band clasped around her wrist. A holographic screen appeared from the Individual Device and other people's lives and opinions filtered into her morning thoughts seamlessly.

A life insurance ad appeared, showing pictures of people falling to the ground in grief after the news of their loved one's death. Calla dismissed it and looked instead at a video of a disgruntled woman slapping a man while the song "Beat the Man Down" by Fig Lady played. The woman yelled in despair over the man's disloyalty in hick soprano. Calla scrolled on, seeing the familiar face of her sister. Her sister held a small child in her arms while her husband kissed her face. Beneath the photo was a sponsorship by the National Marriage Council. Calla dismissed the screen and crawled out of bed. Her feet touched the cold floor as she scampered to get ready to visit her parents.

On the train, Calla motioned her I.D. screen out, glancing at fellow passengers who seemed to be staring off into space. Of course she couldn't see other people's I.D. screens, the techstamp tattooed on her wrist beneath her device ensured only she could see hers. It certified that her device would know her. It confirmed her identity.

She scrolled through peoples' posts and stopped at an ad. "BioCompanion: proven by science to find your one true love." Calla thought of her cold, empty apartment. How lonely and silent it always was. Over the past few months, she found herself stirred more and more by the idea of having someone to share life with. She clicked on the ad and a video started.

A woman about the same age as Calla appeared, seated in a living room. "Do you ever feel like you're all alone in the world? That no one understands or notices you? Well, there are so many just like you, feeling lost and alone in today's world. Let BioCompanion help you find that one in 8.5 billion. The one person who is chemically and biologically suited for you. How can chemistry and biology find you love, you ask? Well, when you buy BioCompanion and go to your local updated techstamp kiosk to get our newly developed BioCompanion tattoo, not only will we match you by location, interests, and hobbies but also on a psychological and biophysical level. BioCompanion will upload a small sample of your blood and find your perfect match. It's pain free and proven to work! Just ask me, that's where I found the love of my life." The woman turned as a handsome man appeared beside her. They hugged and smiled back at Calla. "Join today, Calla!" the couple said in unison.

Calla saved the link to her I.D. and dismissed her screen before exiting the train. She saw the merit in having someone she could talk to and share secrets and news with—someone who was still alive and in the real world. She decided she would ask her parents about it. She purchased the usual single rose bloom from the flower stand outside the cemetery walls, scanned her I.D., and gained access to the mausoleum. Pausing at the small plaque with the names Eugene Ripley and Sally Ripley, she said, "Hello, Mom. Hi, Dad." A screen flickered over the names and an elderly couple appeared.

"Calla, it's so nice to see you," her mom said, smiling.

"Did you bring your mom a rose today?" her dad asked.

"I did. This one is yellow," Calla paused, sniffing the bloom. "It smells nice."

"Oh, thank you, dear," her mom said. "But you know you don't have to keep bringing them."

"I know," Calla said. Calla took the old wilted rose she had placed above their plaque the week before and replaced it with the new yellow one.

"Have you made any new friends?" her dad asked.

Calla put her hand on the screen where the projections of her parents lived. "I miss you guys so much," she said.

"Oh, Calla. You seem lonely," her mom said softly.

"I'm not lonely, I have you guys," Calla said, wiping a tear from her cheek. She knew it was a lie. She was always happy to talk with her parents, yet she felt a growing sense of isolation, always separated from the present, not seeing, touching, or talking to anyone living in the same place and time as she.

"You visit us every week, but you know this isn't really us," her dad said. "This is just a representation of us."

"I know…" Calla said, trying not to accept it. The questionnaire her parents took before their deaths was uploaded into A.I. that in turn mimicked their personalities. Sometimes Calla tried to forget, and imagined they were merely separated by distance, ignoring the fact that she stood before their graves.

"What do you want to talk about today? New TV shows?"

"I think I might try an app to help me find someone," Calla said. "I…I am lonely. I didn't really realize it until the train ride over here."

"You mean find romance?" her mom said, lighting up.

"What do you all think?"

"We have no doubt that you'd be able to find love," her mom said.

"Take a chance," her dad added.

Calla felt energized by the words of her onscreen parents. This version of them always offered their blessing. Never contradicting, never chastising, never raising their voices. She thought she remembered her mother always biting her lower lip, anticipating bad news whenever Calla had something important to say. And it seemed Calla's dad had usually grunted and groaned his advice, as though he knew Calla wouldn't really be paying attention to what he had to say. But these entities created for her never did these things, and the ease of conversation with them now seemed more familiar to her than the fading memories of the imperfect human versions.

Calla left her parents' gravesite and walked the street toward the train. She stopped near a techstamp kiosk. She decided to take a chance. Calla opened the door to the machine and went inside the booth, closing and locking the door behind her. She took a sanitary cloth from her pocket and wiped the screen inside the kiosk. The room was sanitized automatically after every use, but Calla still felt the grunge of use inside the little room. She opened her I.D. screen and bought and downloaded the BioCompanion app.

"Welcome to BioCompanion!" a woman's voice spoke. "You're on your way to true, everlasting love. Just search for the BioCompanion app at your local up-to-date techstamp kiosk. A blood sample will be required to find your BioCompanion. Then you can install your tattoo and scan it to your I.D. to get started today!"

Calla tapped the kiosk screen and searched BioCompanion, clicking on the name when it appeared. "Where would you like your techstamp today?" the machine asked. A row of tattoo location options appeared on the kiosk screen.

Calla clicked on forearm. "Choose your design," the machine announced. There were ink black, pure white, electric blue, or varied skin color options. Calla chose a skin color option which she thought would blend in with her natural skin tone. A holographic square appeared in front of her, its border neon green, hovering in place. "A blood sample is required for this app before your techstamp is installed. Do you consent?"

"Yes," said Calla.

"Please, place your forearm inside the square facing upward."

Calla slowly placed her arm inside the square. "We will begin. Please, stay still." Calla felt a tiny prick and watched as a beam of light floated a small sample of her blood for analysis. "Blood sample complete. Remain still for techstamp installment."

A laser struck her wrist, etching designs on her skin. She felt a slight tickle but still managed to keep still. "Your techstamp is complete. Have a good day," the kiosk announced. Calla inspected her arm. The design of the tattoo was a subtle heart with squared edges. Smaller lines imitated the shape like a target getting smaller toward the center. It blended with her skin well and Calla was happy. She stood and left the kiosk, no longer feeling the cold of the day.

Once home, Calla opened her BioCompanion app with her new techstamp. "Your profile has been successfully made. Please, choose a profile picture." Calla scrolled through her photos and picked one. "You are one step closer to finding love." Calla found she was smiling yet felt a twinge of anxiety in the pit of her stomach. She dismissed the app and pulled up her work tasks for the day, trying to think of other things. Calla worked as a database administrator for a local company using specialized software to organize their data and defend it from any unauthorized users. It wasn't an exciting gig, but she could work from the comfort of her own apartment and it paid the bills. After a full day's work, Calla climbed into bed. She opened the BioCompanion app to see her profile was still pending. She dismissed her screen and turned over in bed, falling into a restless sleep.

A dulcet chime woke Calla. Squinting, she looked at the I.D. on her wrist where a bright, blue light flashed a notification. Calla's breath caught. "It found someone," she whispered to the empty room. She opened the notification with her new techstamp and a man's profile appeared. "Orson Smith." A lump of nervousness collected in her throat as she studied the man's features. His thin lips edged upward to one side in an uneven and forced smile. His eyes seemed hopeless and dark. His hair was a sandy, curly mess that rested over his brows. She thought he had the most endearing features she had ever seen. Unsure how to approach the situation, she started to dismiss her screen when a message appeared.

"Hello, Calla. It's Orson. I know this might be a little forward and awkward, but do you think you'd be interested in meeting tonight?"

Calla sat up in her bed, the glow of the screen casting a pool of light across her covers. Her eyes darted back and forth in thought. "Tonight?" she messaged, looking at the time in the corner of her screen.

"Well, it's only 11 p.m."

"But I'm in bed."

"Me too. But how often do you get to meet your one true love?" A picture of Orson's handsome face lit with a halo of blue light popped up in the message, showing him also in bed.

"That's exactly what I'm doing," she said, sending him a picture of herself. "Where should we meet?"

"Somewhere public so you don't think I'm trying to murder you?"

"I thought I specifically asked this app to filter out murderers."

"LOL. Would you want to meet at The Atlas? Have you been there?" he asked.

"That's my favorite bar."

"Of course it is. See you at 12:15?"

"Okay."

Calla adjusted her blouse nervously as she waited at a table. The Atlas was a bar at the top of one of the tallest buildings in the city. Calla turned from anxiously looking toward the entrance to inspect the city lights below. She rarely went out anymore, but when she did, she went to The Atlas. The lights of the city below gave her a clear and calm feeling; looking at things from above, neatly placed around the streets and organized in rows of sparkling light made life seem more orderly than it actually was.

"Calla?" a voice asked.

Calla turned to see the man from the app. "Orson."

"You look very nice," he said.

Calla's face flushed with heat. "Thanks," she answered.

Orson sat across the table. "So, we have been matched."

"We have," Calla said. "I can't believe it worked so quickly. I only downloaded the app this morning." Her heartbeat quickened as she spoke. She took a deep breath, trying to calm her nerves.

"Really? I've been on the app for months. Never been matched with anyone. So, maybe now you understand my excitement in wanting to meet you so soon. My perfect match."

Calla blushed and met his gaze. "It's okay," she said. "I had nothing going on and don't even have to get up early."

"Relationships have been tough for me. No one seems interested in anything long term anymore. This app promised something more stable. I've been worn thin trying to find the right person and never being able to predict how things will pan out."

"Love can be unpredictable," she said. A drink arrived for Orson and Calla raised the glass she had been slowly sipping while she waited. "To our first meeting."

"To us," Orson said, taking a drink. He turned to look out the window. "Don't you love this view?"

"I do," Calla said, looking out at the city. "It's why I like this place so much. It makes me feel like I'm far away from everything, as if I can be present."

"Like you're disconnected?"

"Exactly."

"It makes me feel like I can see everything I'm part of more clearly, to understand the world below in a new light, to connect with it all better."

"I guess you could look at it that way," said Calla. She examined Orson. His dark eyes reflected the sparkling lights of the city below. He was intended to be her perfect match, a proven match. Yet, he seemed to see the world from her favorite place a little differently. But Calla wanted to leave the world of blurred lines and feeble online connections and try something real, and it seemed like Orson did too. As she looked into his eyes, she found that they were looking into hers. He was living, feeling, and with her in that moment. Her heart leapt.

For weeks Calla and Orson spent every waking moment together. Calla started to believe Orson would stay with her the rest of their lives, securing her happiness and ending her loneliness. But neither Calla nor Orson could predict the future or the human tendency to feel utterly restless, even in happiness.

"Do you think we could ever be truly happy?" Calla asked one night as Orson and she were in bed. "Humans, I mean."

"People weren't made to be happy," Orson answered. "Maybe once we were, when we didn't know any better and the world was green and lush and warm. I used to go days without physically speaking to anyone…yet I don't know if that's what makes me unhappy."

"Isn't our technology supposed to make us happy? Isn't that its job? Artificial intelligence is supposed to make our lives simpler, better. But I don't think we made it smart enough to understand us."

"What do you mean?" Orson asked.

"Well, it shows us things it thinks we want to see. These algorithms and apps show us our interests. Our interests aren't always happy," Calla said.

"Technology brought us together," Orson said. "It can't always make you and I happy, but it can deduce that we are made for each other."

"But," Calla said, turning over on her side to look at Orson, "that doesn't necessarily mean I won't make you completely miserable someday, whether by leaving, not being who you thought, or dying."

Orson looked away. "You're right," he said. "No matter how A.I. tries, we're still part of this world, and it's unpredictable."

"I like the unknown," Calla said, kissing Orson.

"I fear it," Orson said, pulling away. "I fear losing you, losing myself, not knowing what's going to happen tomorrow when I wake up."

"But that's life. Life is unpredictable."

"Maybe it doesn't have to be like that," Orson said.

"What do you mean?"

"Did you know that there was a man who was walking just a few blocks from here who had a hammer fall on his head? One moment he's alive and in a split second everything's done. What if we had a way to stop all that?"

"What, like a way to predict the unknown...predict the probability that a hammer will fall on your head and kill you?"

"Maybe," Orson answered, his eyes turned to Calla but he was no longer looking at her. "We could use A.I. and use others. Connect to each other and see the world at every possible angle. Protecting us from more unknowns because you'd know so much more."

"You mean collective intelligence?" Calla said, with a laugh.

"Don't laugh, Calla," Orson growled, getting to his feet.

"I...I'm sorry. I didn't know you were being serious."

"Well, I am. I've lost so many people. Everyone I love, Calla."

Calla looked down. Orson had lost his parents at a young age and his brother only a few years ago, and every relationship since had been poisoned with betrayal, abuse, and apathy. Calla loved Orson deeply and never wanted to hurt him. "Orson, look at me," she said, getting to her feet and walking over to him. "I love you and always will."

"You don't know that. Already, I'm starting to feel less connected to you than the week before. I want to have you with me always."

"I am here," Calla said. "Right now. I am here. In the past few months, you have made my life so much warmer and happier than ever before. I don't want you to worry about all this uncertainty." She cupped his face in her hands and smiled. Orson managed a grin.

The next morning Calla woke to find Orson had left. She messaged him and he immediately replied, "I have a surprise! I'll be back soon!"

Calla milled around her apartment, ate breakfast, and began checking in on her work duties when Orson returned.

"Calla, I discovered something this morning," he said, as he entered.

"Where have you been?"

"I was meeting with a think tank."

"What?"

"I've been talking to this group online called the Tech Torrents. They got me interested in this new technology. It's going to transform the world, Calla. Save us from the unknown." Orson knelt next to Calla. He opened his palm to reveal a small microchip and smiled up at her.

"What is it?" Calla asked, curious.

"It's a neural sensor," he said.

"Well, loads of people get those. What's special about this think tank's neural uplink?"

"It's paired with everyone on the network. You can see and know their thoughts simultaneously. Your thoughts can live inside others."

"Oh, Orson." A bolt of disbelief shot through Calla's chest and her hand covered her mouth.

"This one is for you," he said. "We never need to feel alone again. We can always feel each other."

"Orson, that's nuts," she said, getting to her feet. "I...I don't want to do that."

"I thought you'd want to be with me like this."

"Orson, that's not what I want, and you wouldn't always like my thoughts, and I know I wouldn't like yours."

"But that's the most beautiful thing about it. We'd never have anything to hide from each other."

"What about privacy? Individuality? And it sounds like it wouldn't just be us. You said this was part of a think tank."

"Yes, the Tech Torrents is what they call it. There's no need for privacy among loved ones."

"Loved ones? I don't know these people," Calla said. "Are you saying you love everyone in this group? Do you even know everyone in this group?"

"Everything is transparent. There are no lies in this world."

"If this has people and A.I. involved, how are we supposed to know what's real and what's a lie set out to make us happy."

"What does it matter how we find happiness?" Orson said.

"A lie never really makes anyone happy because they eventually figure out the truth," Calla said.

"What if we just blissfully lived in some world made up for us. One we never questioned or even tried to understand beyond what seemed real. Wouldn't we be happy then?"

"Yes, but someone else would be very unhappy. Someone would have to know the truth for the lie to work."

"Would you ever disconnect your I.D. for more than a few minutes? Or do you fear what might happen? Don't you fear not having everything at the tip of your fingers? Not knowing something as minuscule as the name of some plant...it might drive you crazy when you've had that power all your life. Knowledge is a scary thing for a person to lose if they know you're taking it, but when you take it from them while they're under the delusion that they know everything, it's bliss. They'll even help you make other people happy the same way. I love you, Calla. But we can never be happy in this world. Not in the capacity we're in. I know it can make us happy. A chance we don't have otherwise."

"I am happy with you, Orson," Calla said, jerking her hand away.

Orson straightened up, smoothing out his shirt with his hands. "They said it takes some people time. I'm willing to wait. If it means protection and connectedness for you."

"Orson, did you get another techstamp?" Calla asked, noticing a tattoo under the collar of his shirt.

"It allows me into their facility."

"Did you become a member of this Tech Torrent group?"

"I am fully committed," he said, his face expressionless.

Over the next few days, Calla began noticing a change in Orson. He grew distant, as though always thinking of something else. Calla knew it must be that he was listening to the thoughts of so many others, trying to find patterns in the chaos. He always seemed deep in thought and his words grew few. Calla felt hopeless, as though the love of her life was falling into a world she did not understand. Until one day, he stopped speaking altogether.

Orson began escaping the apartment they shared. He would leave without a word, even when Calla begged for an answer. She struggled to awake Orson from the delusion of happiness in the torrent of his mind. Then, Orson left the apartment and never returned. There was no reply when Calla tried to message him. She searched for a physical note, some sign or answer to his disappearance, but only found the neural sensor he had gotten for her resting on her nightstand.

Calla walked alone. She purchased the usual single rose bloom from the flower stand outside the cemetery walls, scanned her I.D., and gained access to the mausoleum. She paused at the small plaque with the names Eugene Ripley and Sally Ripley. "Hello, Mom. Hi, Dad," she said. A screen flickered over the names and her parents appeared.

"Calla, it's so nice to see you," her mom said.

"Did you bring your mom her rose?" her dad asked.

"I did. This one is white," she answered, smelling the petals.

"How's your boyfriend? When are we going to meet him?"

"He's good," she said, biting her lower lip. "I think we're going to get married. We want children. I'll have to bring them here someday so they can meet you." Orson had been missing from Calla's life for weeks, but in a world where her parents were perfect and alive, where she was settled and happy, where her future seemed bright and promising, Orson had to be a part of it.

"Oh, that's amazing, sweetheart. We are so happy for you. What a wonderful life you seem to be having."

"Yes, it's wonderful," she said.

"Sweetheart, what is that on your neck?" her dad asked.

Calla placed a hand over her new techstamp. "Oh, it's nothing," she said. "It's just a tattoo I got so I could be with Orson again."

"I thought you were already with Orson, darling," her mom said.

"And I always will be," Calla answered, smiling into the screen on her parents' gravesite plaque.

ORCHIDACEAE

The Carapod ship continued forward, despite Bruno's warning transmission, and cut closer to the human zone. Bruno tried to contact the ship once more. "Turn," he whispered. "Just turn around."

The ship showed no indication of response, forcing Bruno to call his weapons online. "Damn," he said in frustration. "Damn, damn, damn." Bruno had watched so many Carapod ships get destroyed when they crossed into the human zone, but this would be the first time he ordered it. A fair amount of the alien ships would turn around when they detected weapons drawn, but some were more obstinate.

He reached a hand to his collar and pulled out the necklace holding the rock his mother had given him before her death. Bruno had drilled a small hole in the rock and ran a chain through it, so it was always with him. The rock was not exceptionally beautiful—a gray, uninteresting stone with no sheen. Bruno's mother had been killed by the Carapods. She had offered them friendship, and in their savageness, they killed her.

Bruno keyed in the weapons code and fired. The shot hit its mark, obliterating the ship. Where only seconds before there had been the peculiar green glow of the Carapods, now there was nothing but black, empty space. "Nice hit," a toneless voice said over the speaker. Bruno didn't reply.

He forced his mind to recall what his commander had said about the Carapods when he was first assigned his own cruiser at the line: "Carapods are just sacks of pus with vines for arms. They don't feel and think like humans do. They continually try to cross the line because they are drawn in by the lights of our station. They think the light means food.

85

They want to shoot a hole in our station, suck us out into space, and eat our frozen bodies."

Bruno looked at the clock. His shift would be over soon.

He sat back in his chair. The ship was silent but for the monotonous buzz of the engine and the obnoxious and steady dinging of sensors. One detected the steady flow of radiation that was always present in space and the other was from the monitoring station informing him that there was another ship approximately a day away. He clicked the notification and saw that it would be approaching the human zone near his next shift. He hoped it wasn't another Carapod ship, but it always was. He looked out into the black void before him and wished they would stop coming. Why did they never answer? Why had Bruno never seen a Carapod ship try and shoot at them? An alarm rang, signaling his shift was over. He turned his ship around and headed back to the station.

A notification sounded and he glanced down at his screen. His weekly rations were ready for pickup. He docked the ship and headed to his locker. The bright lights of the locker room were always a headache after being in the low-lit interior of his cruiser. Bruno squinted as he unzipped his suit and hung it inside his locker. He slammed the locker shut. The notation B58 gleamed back at him from the nameplate. He looked down the wall of identical lockers and sighed.

Bruno continued to the usual collection dock for his rations. As he approached, a woman glared down at him from her perch in the high window of the collection dock. "Can I help you?" she asked.

"I'm here to collect my rations for the week."

"Name and age?"

"Bruno Foster and I'm 22 years old."

The woman typed his name and then pulled something from a drawer. "Looks like it's your lucky day," she said with no hint of enthusiasm. "Your rations are to be picked up in Section A this week. Here's your temporary entry badge." The woman leaned down and handed him a small plastic ID.

"Section A rations," Bruno said, looking at the badge. "Do you know why?"

"A reward for shooting down your first Carapod ship."

"Oh," Bruno said, nodding. "Thank you." Bruno left the collection area and rounded the corner to the Section A elevator bank. The whir of machinery vibrated underfoot as he stood at the platform. He watched as people trickled out of the metal capsules on their way to work. Section A was the coveted level of the station, where the elite lived in leisure. Section B was where most people worked, including those from Section A. And Section C held all the ductwork and mechanical workings of the massive station. In Section B, there were separate elevator banks for each section. Section B elevators took you to all the different floors on B. There were only four A elevators on Section B, and Bruno had heard they all went to the same level on Section A. He didn't know exactly how many levels Section A had. Bruno had only ever seen Section B. It was where he ate, lived, and undocked and docked his ship for work.

"Excuse me," an old man said, pushing his way around Bruno. The man scanned a badge from his breast pocket and pressed the button for one of the Section A elevators. Bruno cleared his throat and followed suit, scanning his temporary badge and pressing the button. He could feel the old man's gaze. Bruno turned to face the man and noticed he was squinting at the new badge on his chest. "I have a temporary badge," Bruno said.

"Oh," the old man said, startled. "Of course, so sorry." The elevator dinged and opened. "After you," the man insisted, gesturing Bruno forward. Bruno had never been inside one of the Section A elevators. The lighting was soft, and the walls were lined with a smooth, dark wood.

The elevator gently chimed, and the doors opened. A sensational breeze met him as he left. Wood-textured materials lined the walls, and gardens of green and red plants weaved through the open foyer, making Bruno forget he was trapped on a station out in the middle of space. He felt as though he had ventured onto foreign soil.

"Can I help you, sir?" an older woman asked. Her gold-laced overskirt gracefully swiveled over her white jumpsuit as she approached. "I can tell you may be a little lost."

"Do I look that clueless?" Bruno said.

She laughed softly. "It's my job to spot the newbies and help them find where it is they are meant to go."

"Oh, I'm looking to collect my weekly rations."

"Of course," she said, smiling. "Just down that hall and to the right."

Bruno nodded a thanks and headed down the hall. The walls of the hall were made of a thick, glimmering stone. Crystalline veins spread through it like tributaries, stretching the length of the hall. Bruno placed his hand on the wall, tracing one of the crystalline intrusions with his finger as he walked. An almost forgotten but deeply familiar fragrance overcame him. He looked around the corner to see an assortment of tapered flower arrangements, cleverly organized in front of a small shop front. He walked toward the flowers in a daze.

"Can I help you?" a woman asked. She approached, flower stem in hand. She was in her late fifties, yet surprisingly sensual, gliding toward him in a fitted red gown which hung loosely off her shoulders. "I've never seen you around here."

"I, uh," Bruno cleared his throat. "I've never been. Your flowers are incredible."

"I'm glad you like them. Why don't you come in?" she asked, gesturing him toward the entrance of her shop.

Bruno followed her command and was delighted to find more wonderful and colorful plants within.

"Is there anything you find particularly interesting?"

"I didn't know there was a flower shop on the station. I thought everyone just replicated them."

"Well," she said, "most people do, but many people on Section A appreciate the real thing. Do you like the real thing?"

Bruno bent down to feel the leaf of a plant. "How do you tell the difference?" he asked.

"You can't," she said. "Not really. Only an expert can spot the difference."

"How so?" Bruno asked.

"Take this plant, for example," she said, gesturing toward a plant with multiple blooms. She held a bloom between her fingers. "It has tiny imperfections. The petals are slightly speckled with a different color than the rest of the blooms and one of the sepals is not the exact shape as the others."

"Why do you sell something that's not perfect?"

"It's special to some people," she said. "I find it more interesting. What do you think?"

Bruno inspected the plant. Several pink blooms sprouted off a single vine. "What's this one called?"

"Orchidaceae. It's very common."

"Orchidaceae?"

"An orchid. There are many hybrids," she said, waving her hand dismissively.

"So, this plant isn't unique, then," Bruno said, looking up at the woman.

The woman laughed. Her white teeth gleamed out from her red painted lips. "It's true, there are many with the exact look and smell as this particular orchid, but that doesn't mean it can't be unique. I grew it myself. It took love and respect for it to reach this maturity. You could bring this plant home, make it your own, care for it, and carry on the tradition. I don't sell them to just anyone. I worked hard to help this plant survive and don't want any of them going to someone who isn't going to do the same. You can just replicate one if you don't want to care for it, or I could make you an arrangement of fresh cut flowers. If you—"

"I didn't say I wouldn't want to care for it." Bruno returned his attention to the plant. The intricate sprinkles of peppered purple and white and the small fragile center with an inkling of yellow gave the plant a face. "It's unique."

The woman paused. "Yes. That's exactly it," she said. She looked down, her eyes growing distant and thoughtful. "It knows what it is and it won't be changed."

Bruno answered, "For me, it is not ruled by imitation. It is real, even if imperfect, unlike a replicated plant may be. Like a truth I've never noticed before."

"That is an interesting way to look at a flower," she said with an inkling of sadness.

"How much for this orchid?" Bruno inquired. "I like it and I think my wife will too."

The woman's exacting eyes returned to life. "Twenty thousand points," she said.

"Twenty thousand," Bruno sighed. "I'm sorry. As beautiful as it is, I cannot afford it. I'm sorry to have wasted so much of your time." Bruno turned to leave.

"Wait," the woman said, placing a hand on Bruno's arm. "Your necklace. Where did you get it?"

Bruno looked at the rock hanging around his neck and quickly tucked it into his collar. "It was a gift from my mother."

"Ah, and does your mother live here on Section A?"

"No, like most my age, my family died with the Second League, when I was very young, when they were betrayed by the Carapods."

"And you remember her?" the woman asked, looking into Bruno's eyes with interest.

"Not really. But I remember this rock was the last thing she gave me," he replied, continuing toward the door.

"What does it mean to you?" she asked urgently.

Bruno thought for a moment. His mother had been a commander in the Second League. She had sent him a rock from every outpost she visited. The rock around his neck had been from the Carapod planet where she was killed. He was only five years old when it happened, and he struggled to remember her. "It means nothing. It's just a reminder that I had a mother."

She studied him for a moment. "Would you be willing to make a trade?"

Bruno lifted the necklace over his neck and studied it in his hand. His mother had sent him many stones from many worlds. Why had he always worn this one? Was it a reminder of her death, a token of love, or simply something to keep his hatred of the Carapods alive so he could push a button week after week, destroying noncompliant ships? He looked at the plant. It made him happy. What did this rock do other than remind him of loss? "Deal," he said. "My necklace for the plant."

Bruno set the orchid on the dining room table and placed his food rations next to it. The plant already added life to the otherwise dull living quarters.

"I'm going to take care of you," Bruno whispered to the plant.

The door alarm sounded, and Ava entered. "Hello," Bruno's wife said, greeting him with a kiss. "I heard you got your first kill today. Congratulations."

"I was sent to Section A for our rations this week," Bruno replied.

"Section A," Ava said, her voice lifting in praise. "Bruno, that's amazing. I look forward to trying them. We will be eating well this week." Ava paused at the table. "What's that?" she asked, looking at the orchid.

"I thought I'd celebrate by bringing us something new. I got it from a shop in Section A."

"You know you can replicate plants for free, Bruno."

"I know, but this is genuine."

"Bruno," she sighed, "I don't think the real ones even keep their blooms that long, and look, that bloom looks a little off. This must have been a hell of a flower salesman."

"She said blooms can return if you take proper care of it."

"Oh, did she. How much did you pay this woman?"

"Nothing."

"Nothing," Ava repeated suspiciously.

"Well, I gave her my necklace."

"The one with the rock your mother gave you? For this?" Ava said, inspecting the blooms of the orchid. "Are you feeling okay?"

"I feel great," Bruno said with a shrug.

"Well, okay," she said, pausing a moment to look him over. "You must be very proud of your kill today, as am I." Ava grinned and took Bruno's hand, leading him from the dining room "Why don't we get cleaned up for dinner?"

Ava turned on the shower and the couple disrobed. The soft hum of water eased Bruno's mind. He closed his eyes as Ava's soft lips moved down his neck. She quickly ran her hands along his back while guiding him to the water. "Congratulations on your kill." Ava smiled and went to kiss him again.

Bruno halted and pushed away.

"What's wrong?" she asked, wiping a stray wet hair from her eyes.

"Ava," Bruno exhaled, "does it ever bother you?"

"Does what bother me?" she asked.

"When you're working at the monitoring station. Does it ever bother you when you see a ship destroyed?"

"When I detect a ship approaching, my reward is when people like you are there to greet it. Until they are dealt with, my concern is that they will harm this station or harm you."

"But why do they never respond? Or shoot at us?"

"Is this really what you want to talk about right now?" she said, pushing back a strand of his hair.

"I don't feel right about it," he said.

"About what?" Ava leaned away.

"We blow them up, but we don't know why. Today, what I did…the ship I destroyed wasn't doing anything."

"Don't know why? Bruno, these creatures killed your mother. They killed my parents. They attack and ask questions later. That's why they don't answer. They don't care to. They want to destroy us, not talk to us."

"Then why don't they ever shoot first?" he asked.

"I'm sure if given the chance they would," she said. "Now, let's change the subject. What was Section A like?"

"It was amazing," Bruno answered, morosely. "But no one our age lives there."

"It takes time to work your way to Section A. Maybe we'll get to live there someday with our children," she said, leaning into him.

"I saw no children there. All the children live here on Section B."

"Well, Section A does seem to be more of a place to retire or lead from. Many of our leaders don't have children because they reserved all their time for taking care of threats to the station. You know that. But maybe we'd be the first to do both."

Bruno smiled at Ava. "That sounds like a lot of work. I don't think it's been done before."

"Don't you want children with me?" she asked.

"Very much."

"I love you, Bruno. You shouldn't feel guilty about protecting us."

"I love you too, Ava," he replied, holding her close.

Bruno watered his orchid and headed into work. He knew he had another encounter with a Carapod ship to look forward to, but he had no choice but to do his job. He went to his locker, pulled his suit on, and headed to his ship. A notification from Ava dinged on his screen. He opened it. "Last night was amazing. Have a nice day at work! Only seeing one ship on the scanners today. Maybe someone else will get it."

It gave Bruno an ounce of comfort to know that Ava was watching him from the monitoring station. She knew he was having concerns about shooting the ships and that worried her. He knew he couldn't share his anxieties with anyone else. He was a soldier, not a philosopher. He was trained to kill, not to think. He was a product, not a source. Bruno thought back to Section A and all its glory. He wondered if he and Ava would ever get to live there. They could have a room full of real plants. He could grow them himself. "Ship approaching," he heard a voice over the radio say.

A dull pain ate at the core of Bruno's insides as he waited. Slowly, the faint green speck of a Carapod ship came into view. He reached toward the com to call it but stopped. What was the point? They never heard his calls. He called his weapons online and rested his fingers over the code panel and waited. Silence filled the air. The ship continued toward him. The Carapod ship approached human space. Bruno sighed and typed in the weapon code. "Hello," a scratchy voice sounded over the silence. Bruno looked to his video screen. An image flickered in and out of view. "Hell…ooo," the voice rang through the static.

Bruno froze, watching the image come into view. "Mom!" he gasped.

"This is Commander Danielle Foster," she said, fading in and out. "I've come to get my son." Her voice was shaky and angry.

"Mom!" he called over the speaker. "Mom, it's me. It's Bruno."

"Bruno," she began to cry. "Bruno, is that really you? We must have finally broken through."

"Yes, it's me," he answered.

"Listen to me," she croaked. "You need to get out. This station. It's not what you think. Section C…" her voice cut out. "Can you hear—"

There was a loud rumble and his mother's image froze. Bruno looked up to see the ship was gone. Another cruiser guarding the line spiraled past and around him.

"Mom," he whispered, looking back down at the screen. The screen was black.

"Bruno?" he heard a voice over the speaker. "Are you okay? You let that ship cross the line. We had to send another ship in front of you to take it out."

The uncomfortable glow of the lights on Section B made Bruno grimace as he placed his suit back into his locker. Hallucination. It had been a hallucination and he just needed time away from the front line. A week would maybe do it. He made his way back to his living quarters and sat at the table. He stared at his orchid and wondered where the species came from. He imagined its ancestors would have never thought their progeny would be on a space station in the middle of nowhere.

He tried to think back to the last memory of his mother but couldn't recall anything before she left to explore the colonies with the Second League. He held a vague idea of how she looked and sounded, but now he only saw the image of her flickering from his cruiser screen and heard only the static-infused voice from the com.

He heard Ava enter. He quickly straightened and steeled himself. "Bruno," she panted as though she had run all the way from work. "What happened?" she asked. She squatted down next to him and placed her hands on his knees.

"What are people saying?" he asked.

"They said you must not be getting enough sleep. They think you need rest. A break."

Bruno leaned toward Ava. "I thought I heard my mother," he whispered.

"What do you mean?" she asked.

Bruno shook his head. "She…she was on that ship. I swear I talked to her. I saw her on the screen."

"What?"

"She said I needed to get out of here."

"I don't understand," Ava breathed. "You're saying your mom was on the Carapod ship?"

"Do you think I'm going crazy?" he asked, his head down, barely touching Ava's shoulder.

"I don't know," Ava answered, holding him in her arms.

"She said something about Section C," he said.

"Why?" Ava asked.

"I don't know," Bruno said.

"Well," Ava sighed. "I think you need to stay home for a few days. You have the time saved up. That doesn't mean trips to the flower shop or Section C, okay? I need you to be sharp. For me," she said and gently touched his face. "And for everyone on the station."

Bruno nodded and headed to their bedroom to rest but sleep never came. Bruno wrestled with the thoughts that breezed through his mind. The vision of his mother's face on the screen was scattered and blotted, but there was no mistaking her face, and her voice—in an instant coming in so crisp and clear. He felt her concern and fear. She was trying to warn him about something to do with Section C. What was in Section C?

Bruno sat up and looked over at Ava's sleeping form. She rarely slept, but when she did there was no waking her, and he didn't want to. He didn't want to bring her into this.

What if he was just imagining it all and what if he was caught? It was best to let her sleep. He gently placed the covers over her shoulders and gave her a soft kiss. He dressed and left the room. He reached into the coat closet to get his jacket and glanced at his orchid. A single flower had severed itself from the plant; it rested all alone on the table. Bruno took the bloom in his hands. He felt silly now, trading his mother's necklace for the thing, yet he still found comfort in knowing it would be here for Ava, if for some reason he was detained for entering Section C without the proper authorization. He placed the fallen bloom inside his pocket and left his home.

He had heard stories of Section C. The stories, however, were never remarkably interesting. It was a place filled with ducts, machinery, and all the internal workings of a space station that the people living in the station didn't want to see. Only people who knew how to work on such things were ever allowed down. He didn't know anyone personally who had to make trips to the lower section. There was only one elevator to Section C and you had to have a badge. It was rarely in use, and it would be hard to bum a ride down. There were a few stairwells that led to Section C, but again, Bruno would need a badge. He knew of only one option—the trash. The rubbish pit was said to dump into Section C. He knew that contemplating using it meant that he was going a bit nutty, but he had to try. He would never be able to forget his mother's words in his cruiser. "It's not what you think…Section C."

The Section B foyer was mostly deserted, and Bruno tried not to draw attention to himself. He approached the trash duct and looked around. No one was looking. He pulled the handle and opened it. A terrible smell escaped, and Bruno coughed. His eyes watered as he inched one leg in and then slowly positioned himself to step in. He held his breath and let himself slide. The sudden exhilaration of falling overwhelmed him. He fell through a rancid darkness, unable to discern his surroundings. A light appeared below him and then Bruno could see the large pile of rubbish. With a slosh, he crashed into the waste. His lungs refused to take in the rotten air. The putrid smell stung, forcing him up with urgency. He searched feverishly for a way out and spotted a door. Trying not to pass out, he smacked against the door. Then Bruno pressed a red button and it slid open. He plunged through to the other side, catching his breath. The stench remained in a diluted form on his clothes and body. He looked ahead and found that he was in a long dark hall. He walked down the passage, slow and cautious. He came to an unmarked fork and paused, looking left and right. The faint sound of voices came echoing from the right hall. He took a step back and peered around the bend.

"It's just this way," a distant voice said.

"I've never been to Section C," another voice said cheerfully. "I thought it might look a little like this, though."

"Just wait, it'll surprise you."

The voices faded and Bruno followed. He saw an older man and woman walking with a younger woman. The older two were elegantly dressed while the youngest wore the garb most commonly seen on Section B. They approached a pair of ornate metallic doors at the end of the hall. The great doors towered twelve feet high, meeting the ceiling. They were light blue and glowed, and swirls of gold moved around their surface like living vines.

"What's this?" the young woman asked.

"Come," the man said. "We'll show you." The man held a key up to the doors and golden tendrils reached out and took it. The doors opened. Bruno bolted to reach them before they closed and the golden vines snaked out at him as he snuck through. The three were just ahead and Bruno dodged behind a large pillar to conceal himself. The room looked as though it were encapsulated in gray stone, yet the pillar Bruno rested against was soft and moist. He looked around the pillar to see the three standing in front of a great gaping hole at least 20 feet wide and 50 feet tall. Bruno squinted but only saw darkness within.

"What's going on?" the young woman asked.

"We have come to pay penance to the Grand Master of the Stars," the older woman announced.

"Master of what?" the young woman stopped, her happiness and warmth draining away.

Bruno froze. His eyes fixed on the opening. A massive gray face slowly emerged from the opening, covered with a thick plating of exoskeleton that shielded its eyes in shadow. A large undulating sack trailed behind its head like a bun. It sloshed forward and slowly held itself up on two sword-like legs. Bruno held a hand over his mouth to keep from crying out in fear.

Silence and horror filled the room, until the old man broke it with hoarse admiration. "Praise the old one," he sang. "Here is our offering. You provide us with wealth and life, and we are forever your humble servants." The old man and woman knelt, and the creature let out a guttural sound of approval, which shook the room and forced Bruno to his knees. The creature lifted a sword leg. The young woman shrieked as the creature stuck the leg through her body. Its shielded face fractured, showing a soft tissue underneath where hideous sharp fangs dripped pink sludge from their pointy tips.

Bruno closed his eyes and covered his ears as the creature ate, but the sound of cracking bone pierced through. His nerve broke. He ran to the door and pushed it open with all his strength, dodging the slithering golden vines as he ran through. He hoped the old couple were too engrossed in their ritual to see him leave. He sprinted down the hall in the direction he had seen the trio come and soon found a door. There was no lock or entry pad on the door, and he pulled it open, rushing up the stairs before he collapsed at the foot of a door labeled Section B.

Bruno hovered over Ava as she slept. Her eyes fluttered open and her hand instinctively covered her face. "Bruno," she gasped. "What is that smell?"

"Ava, there's a monster living on Section C."

"What? Bruno, where have you been?"

"I think people on Section A are using us to feed it. It must give them something, but I'm not sure what."

"Bruno, you're talking crazy," Ava said, holding her nose. "You need to calm down. I don't understand."

"We need to get out!" Bruno cried. He reached down and took her by the shoulders.

"You're scaring me."

"You should be scared," he said, shaking her. "We should all be scared. They are killing people, Ava."

"There's a monster in Section C?"

"Is there another ship coming today?"

"A ship?" Ava paused. "You mean a Carapod ship?"

"My mother was on the last ship. We killed her!" Bruno fell to his knees. "I'm certain of it. I know in my gut. I think those ships aren't what they seem. Aren't what we've been told."

"Bruno, please." Ava inched her way off the bed toward her husband. She pulled him toward her, even though he knew he reeked.

Bruno held her tight as he began to cry. "Do you love me?" he asked.

"I love you very much," she said.

"Then please trust me. I know it sounds mad. But I saw it with my own eyes," he said.

"I just want to help you," Ava replied. "I've never seen you like this."

"Is there a ship coming today?" he asked.

"Yes, there was one. It's supposed to approach," Ava paused, looking toward a clock, "in about an hour."

"I've got to help it pass through the zone."

"What?" Ava got to her feet. "Bruno, you've lost it."

"No, I think I finally understand something. Ava, I love you and I have to do this if either of us is ever going to be free."

"Free. What are you talking about?"

"I've got to go." Bruno stood and kissed Ava.

"But," Ava pushed away, "what are you going to do?"

Bruno turned and walked from the room. Ava followed and they both paused at the front door. "Please," Bruno said, placing his hand on the doorknob, "try and listen when the time is right. Will you be at the monitoring station? Will you go there when the ship arrives?"

"Yes." Ava looked at her watch. "My shift starts in 30 minutes."

"I love you, Ava," Bruno said before leaving.

Bruno felt as though the world had slowed down. He walked toward the docking area to collect his ship. He could hear every beat of his heart. It overpowered the other senses. People stopped and stared at him as he walked by, but he heard no gasps or inquiries over the smell of trash that lingered on his person. His mind only allowed one thought in. He needed to let the next Carapod ship pass the human zone and get its message through to the monitoring station.

He arrived at the docking area and opened his locker. He reached for his suit and began taking off his trash-stained clothes. He felt in his pocket and found the orchid bloom. Slightly limper, but still beautiful. He placed the bloom to his nose and smelled its floral fragrance. He stepped into his suit and clipped the bloom to his collar with a pin he found in his locker.

He detached his cruiser from the outer hull of the station and headed into open space. A message from Ava appeared on his screen. "Bruno, please come back. I don't understand."

Bruno selected reply. "You will. Please. Listen today," he typed.

A sensor began alerting Bruno of an approaching ship. Bruno increased his thrust to meet it.

Ava stood at her post on the observation deck, wringing her hands as she watched her husband's ship grow small.

"I thought Bruno was taking the week off?" a colleague asked.

"Oh," she said, clearing her throat, "you know Bruno can never take a day off." Her insides knotted and she called up her screen. Ava zoomed in on her husband's ship and waited.

"Looks like he's got another," a voice said. "I guess we should hold the other ships back if he's certain he's taking it. I hope he doesn't muck this one up."

"He won't," Ava replied, unable to keep her eyes from the screen. As the Carapod ship approached Bruno's ship began turning perpendicularly.

"What the hell is he doing?" someone asked.

"Bruno," Ava whispered. "What are you doing?"

"The ship is about to enter our zone!" someone yelled. "Ava, tell him to shoot!" Ava held her ground, listening for Bruno. They continued, "It's getting closer. We need to shoot it down, but Bruno's ship is in the way."

"Just wait," Ava commanded. She leaned in, listening. A low buzz emitted through the speakers, but there was only silence. She thought about all the times they had tried to contact the Carapods. They never responded. She always thought they were stupid or vindictive, but now her husband was gambling his life to see if they would speak.

She quickly scanned the room and found the communications console unattended. Her boss usually stood guard at the console. It was his station and not to be touched. But right now he was probably enjoying a long breakfast in Section A. It meant losing her job if she was caught, but Ava dashed to the console and opened the screen. She scrolled through the menu and found her evidence. Incoming communication was set to "off," blocking all incoming calls from reaching the station from outside the zone. Ava's heart dropped. "Why…why are we blocking their communications?" she asked, looking around the room. Her colleagues exchanged bewildered looks.

Ava switched incoming communications to "on." A patter of static sounded and quickly faded. "This is Commander CJ Marks with the Second League," a voice emitted through the speakers. "If you can hear me, children, this is not your world. You are being used. Bred for slaughter. There is a Carapod leader on Section C of your station. The others, the elders on your ship, they are giving you up as its food in return for the great healing power the Carapod leader possesses. We are the Second League marooned with only old fleets of Carapod cruisers. We cannot get far in them. The others have taken all of you from us. You are our only hope of escape and this message is the only hope you have of the truth. Please, you need to get out while you still can."

"What?" someone in the room gasped. "Is that coming from the Carapod ship?"

"What did it say?" another voice asked.

Ava stared out at her husband's ship; tears began obscuring the view. Suddenly, there was a flash and Bruno's ship disintegrated. "No," Ava gasped, clutching the console to keep herself from falling. The ship Bruno was blocking quickly zipped away, escaping. Ava turned to see her boss standing over a control panel.

"It seems we have traitors among us," he said, shaking his head. The others looked at him severely.

"Did he just shoot Bruno's ship down from here?" a woman asked.

"How?" another said.

"Did you hear what the voice said?" Ava asked. Her voice was steady despite the tears streaming down her face.

"Yes," he sighed, "and what a horrible lie."

"A lie?" someone shouted.

Ava's rage swelled. She approached her boss and struck him in the face. "You are the liar," she spat. The old man held his face and gave her seething glare—a small smear of blood smudged across his chin. Two large men burst through the doors of the observation deck.

"Take her to her quarters until we decide what to do with her," he said. The others protested as the men took hold of Ava and dragged her from the room. She was escorted through the halls of the ship and thrown inside her and Bruno's living quarters. Ava fell to the floor. She looked up to see the orchid plant Bruno had brought home. A single bloom fell to the floor next to her. She collected the bloom in her hands and anger coursed through her veins. She knew the truth. Everyone knew it. Bruno had died for the truth and it was time to face it.

THE HALL OF CHRISTMAS

In 1477, four hundred Burgundian soldiers froze to death on Christmas Eve under Charles the Bold's command while awaiting battle at Nancy.

In 1940, Germany bombed the city of Manchester during World War II. The event became known as the Manchester Blitz or Christmas Blitz.

In 1968, the crew of the Apollo 8 mission reached lunar orbit and gave a live broadcast from orbit on Christmas Eve, quoting from the book of Genesis.

In 2303, a renowned human historian died of complications from cancer, which was most likely brought on by his prolonged exposure to radiation while analyzing artifacts on Earth's surface.

The crunching of snow echoed through the empty forest path. The bitter night wind stung Henry's face as he rode. His horse, Mercury, was as smooth and sleek as her namesake, cutting through the darkness with precision.

"Heave on! Heave on!" Henry yelled, holding his lustrous sword up high. Mercury picked up speed, snorting moist plumes of vapor from her flaring nostrils. "Faster now, faster! They'll show soon enough." Henry peered through the visor of his metal armet. The thick armor soaked up the cold, making it more than the man-at-arms could bear. His eyelashes began to freeze, his hands were numb, and his feet grew painful in the stirrups. Whiteness began creeping over his consciousness. A growing internal haze made it hard to focus on his goal at present. He shook himself awake. "It is the eve of Noël," he whispered. "God willing, I shall prevail."

There was a jarring crack and a thud, and Henry found himself among the frozen snowdrifts. He lifted the helmet from his head to see Mercury's hind end fade in the distance. "No, you stubborn nag! Come back!" The sound of snow cracking under her hooves diminished until only silence filled the night. A chill rose in Henry's bones. He unstrapped his pauldrons and staggered ahead before falling in confusion. "To hell with that horse," he said through chattering teeth. "I am lost."

Henry turned over on his back to face the night sky. Tiny luminous specks floated in the sea of black above. The heavens were all a mystery to him. If he could do things over again, he would have been a man of science, a man of great thought, someone who found beauty in life, not one who followed any great lord to war at every bid. If only he had spent more time in thought and writing, but his life had been a grim existence. All the battles he'd seen, the men he'd killed, and the violence he'd witnessed every day since he could remember flashed before him. "Let me think of joyous things for my last moments of memory, oh Lord," he pleaded to the snowy night. "Oh, how I hope for a future of peace. One where the young do not see man's blood flow so freely by another man's doing. If I could see God's will at work years from now, I pray that they would not know the atrocities that I have known. That will be my last request. My last Christmastide wish."

Henry hugged his arms in and prepared to meet eternity when music awoke him from his frigid slumber. Finding new hope in the mysterious sound, Henry slowly rose. He lurched through the icy trees, until a great hall appeared. He knew then, upon seeing it, just how lost he'd become in the snow. The window slits were lit and shining as though a dozen fine lords and ladies were dining within its grand interior.

Henry reached the tall door and rattled the knocker. "I am Henry, man-at-arms for Charles the Bold," he announced feverishly. When there was no reply, Henry became angry and afraid. If he couldn't get into warmth and shelter, it would mean death, so he opened the great door.

Inside, he found there were no great fires or feasts. The palace was dark, lit only by beams of moonlight filtering through slits in the walls. Yet, the music played on. It was a strange tune. The sound frightened him. He reached for his sword only to find it missing. The weapon must have fallen from his grasp earlier on the path.

Henry searched the walls for anything with which he might defend himself but found nothing. He continued to walk toward the music and turned into a great hall. He stopped at the sight of a young tan-skinned woman dancing in the center of the room. She moved freely through the moonlight. "A witch," he whispered. His throat tightened. The woman wore trousers and not the dress of a lady. Her dance was unlike any he had ever beheld, and her clothes were absurd. He knew he should feel outraged and report her for witchcraft, but there was something about her he liked. Henry found he envied her. Instead of hatred, he found long- ing in his heart. Not desire toward the woman herself, but toward some knowledge she seemed to possess, some mys- tery only she knew. If he had been born a great lord, he may still never have known the freedom the woman seemed to hold. It was a freedom of expression. The woman stopped abruptly and turned toward him. Henry was both intrigued and frightened at her gaze.

She looked Henry over in surprise and spoke to him in a language he did not understand.

"I am Henry, man-at-arms for Charles the Bold, Duke of Burgundy. You must know that it is a mortal sin for a woman to wear men's clothing!"

The woman studied him a moment before speaking. "You are French," she said in his native tongue. "Are you alright? Do you live nearby? Have you been hiding long?"

"I am Burgundian! And I do not hide. Witch!"

"Witch?" she laughed. "Why are you dressed so funny? Christmas party?"

"Do you mock the livery of a soldier?"

The woman's face grew ashen. "I'm so sorry," she said. "Would you like something to eat? I have Christmas cakes. You are welcome to them." She turned and suddenly seemed confused. "I…I—they were right here. I was…I was home, but now…where am I?"

"Are you trying to trick me?" Henry growled.

"No," she answered frantically. "I was home and suddenly I'm not. Who are you?"

"I have already told you. I am Henry—"

"Oh, yes. Henry Charles something."

"No, Henry with Charles the Bold—"

"How did I get here, Henry? I was in my home making Christmas biscuits and cakes and now I'm in this strange place."

"I do not know how you got here. I have only just entered and have seen you here."

"I remember hearing the alarm. Yes, oh God," her voice lowered, "I heard the warning."

"Warning? What warning?"

"I was listening to the radio and then I heard it. I knew I should have been underground, but I wanted to make something special. It wasn't like it was turkey or anything, just a few sweets. It wasn't going to take long." The woman paused a long moment and Henry could see the shimmer of tears on her bronze cheek. "I am dead," she said. "I am dead or dreaming."

"No, not dead," Henry said, trying to recall his own journey to the great hall.

"Dreaming, then? And you are in my dream? A knight in my dream; that would make sense."

"You are in mine," he answered. The woman walked closer, placing a hand on his cheek as if to test his realness. A sudden vision of explosions and fire flared in Henry's mind. Great silver birds soared across a dark sky, dropping fire and devastation under their shimmering bellies. He stumbled back in terror, meeting the young woman's eyes.

"What did you see?" the woman asked.

"Fire, so much fire and…heat."

"I saw ice and snow. Men frozen in ice and snow."

"What could it mean?" Henry asked.

"I don't know—" A burst of wind overtook the hall and the two ran for cover in the far corner of the room.

"What's happening?" the woman shouted.

"Some sort of dark magic!" Henry yelled.

A cyclone of snow formed in the center of the room, growing in width and height until it reached the ceiling of the enormous hall. Henry closed his eyes, expecting to be overcome by the blizzard. But everything fell silent and he opened his eyes to see a mighty fir tree in the center of the room. The tree was decorated with colorful figurines and twinkling lights on string. The room grew warm and comfortable and Henry looked to the woman beside him. "Is this Heaven?" he asked.

"I don't know," she said, getting to her feet. "Punch!" she cried, running toward a large bowl of red liquid. "Come, try it!" She offered a small pour for Henry.

The drink was exemplary, and Henry felt warmed. "I have never tasted anything so sweet or seen a tree decorated in such a way."

"Oh, look, Christmas biscuits, and cakes!" Despite not having any explanation for the existence of the feast, Henry found himself giddy with the pleasure of food and drink. But his companion's face soon turned downcast and he stopped his merrymaking.

"What is your name?" he asked the woman.

"Jane Thompson."

"Jane, does any of this make sense to you?"

"No." Jane's face grew graver. "I was home in England when I found myself here with you. I don't know where or when I am, but it still seems to be Christmas Eve."

"Why do you say 'when'?"

"I don't know, to be honest. What I do know is that it was 1940, and whatever place this is most certainly is not that year."

"1940," Henry gasped. "Is this true?"

"Yes," Jane answered.

"I am from the year fourteen hundred and seventy-seven."

116

"Well, that explains the whole witch business earlier."

"I do not understand."

Jane walked to the tree and examined its magnificent branches. "Do you hear that?" she asked.

Henry paused, listening to the faint mumble of someone speaking. "Through there," he said, pointing to a door across the hall. The two moved carefully toward the voices and opened the door. Before them, a box gleamed with movement and light. Henry froze in bewilderment. "What is it?"

"A television," Jane answered. "I've never seen one in person." Jane's eyes grew wide and Henry looked to the contraption.

"What is the thing saying?" he asked.

"There's a man saying they are approaching lunar sunrise," she said, inching closer to the screen. "He says, 'For all the people back on Earth, the crew of Apollo 8 has a message that we would like to send to you. In the beginning...'" Tears began to fall from Henry's eyes as Jane quoted from the Book of Genesis, which he knew well.

"...and there was light," he said, quietly saying the words with her as she translated.

Jane stopped in astonishment. "These men are in space. I don't understand what they're looking at. He said lunar sunrise." Jane inched closer to the television.

"What do you mean?" Henry loomed over the box of moving light, seeing a picture of a grainy slice of rock surrounded by a world of black. "What is this?"

"I'm not sure...but they are saying it's the moon."

"The moon," Henry repeated. "That sliver of gray in a sea of blackness?" he said, pointing to the screen.

"Yes, the blackness being outer space," Jane said. "In the sky…beyond Earth."

"They have reached the heavens," he answered.

"Yes."

"Then…it must be a future of peace."

"No," said Jane, pointing to a paper on the floor. "It's a newspaper. It's dated 1968." She rustled the paper in her hands. "War in Vietnam." She turned the page toward Henry. "It's not all stars and sunshine."

Henry took the paper from Jane and saw a bleak picture of destruction and chaos. "War still," he said grimly. "Will there always be bloodshed?"

"What's that?" a raspy voice broke in, speaking muddled French.

Henry instinctively reached for his sword, but again the weapon was missing, and he soon realized it was not needed. An elderly man rose from the chair in the corner of the room.

"Have you been there this whole time?" Jane asked, turning in surprise.

"I only just arrived," answered the old man.

"Who are you?" Henry asked.

"My name is Timothy."

"Is this your home, Timothy?" Jane asked.

"No." The old man looked about the room. He shuffled toward the couple and took the paper from Henry's hand. "Ah, yes," the old man said, inspecting the newspaper. "Will there always be bloodshed? I heard you ask this question only moments ago. And in French. Are you both French?"

"I am English," Jane answered.

"Ah, I can…speak it too," Timothy said in English. "But it's been…a very, very long time." He returned to French, asking, "What are your names?"

"Jane Thompson and this is Henry…of, uh, Burgundy."

"Most interesting," the old man said, turning to look at the television.

Henry and Jane stepped back in fear. A horrid mess of mangled skin and hair covered the backside of the old man's skull.

"What happened to you?" Henry asked.

"Oh, yes," the old man said with a smile. "My scars. Old battle wounds. They look like hell, but I assure you they stopped hurting long ago." He turned his attention back to the television. "I've always wanted to see this broadcast. All footage of it has been lost."

"Lost?" Jane shook her head, confused.

"Yes," the old man said.

"Are they in outer space?" Jane asked.

"The men of the Apollo 8 mission orbited the moon. They were the first humans to reach it."

"And all footage of it is lost?" Jane asked.

"A great deal has been lost. New histories were written…many accounts lacking truth. History became a subject for shifting blame and no longer one of truth. I aimed to stop that. To search for hard evidence of the past."

"That is how you know about Apollo 8?" Jane asked.

"Yes, I spent my life dedicated to the histories of humanity. I believe it ended up killing me."

"Where are you from?" Henry asked.

"Oh, that's a loaded question in my time."

"You're from the future," Jane said.

"I am not from this time. As I understand neither of you to be." Timothy made a discerning gesture at their clothing.

"Does something horrible happen in the future?" Jane asked.

"Where are you from Jane?" Timothy asked.

"Manchester…1940."

"And you ask me if something horrible has happened? What about you, Henry of Burgundy…I suppose I should ask you what year you are from?"

"Fourteen hundred and seventy-seven," Henry said, standing at attention.

"That is interesting. I know very little of that time on Earth. I am from 2303."

"So far in the future," Jane gasped.

"You have seen many battles in your time?" Henry asked.

"Oh, yes," Timothy answered. "Ever since I can remember."

"That is not what I wished," Henry said.

"What did you wish?" Jane asked.

"When I thought I was about to die, I wished for a future of peace. I prayed that children would never know the atrocities that I have known. It was my Christmastide wish. I have now lost all hope of that dream."

"Don't lose hope, Henry," Jane said, taking his hand in her own. "Hope is the most human thing I can think of." There was a vibration, and the three exchanged questioning looks.

"What is outside this room?" Timothy asked.

"There is a great hall fit for a Christmas ball," Jane said.

The Hall of Christmas

Timothy walked between Henry and Jane toward the door and stopped. "This is no hall of Christmas."

"What do you mean?" Jane asked, exchanging a look with Henry. The two walked to where the old man stood and looked out the door. Where there had been a large fir tree and an extravagant spread of Christmas treats, there was a room with a large window looking out onto a bright light.

"What is it?" Henry asked.

"I...I do not know," replied Timothy, stepping over the threshold toward the window.

"This brightness brings me to search a memory," Henry said.

"Yes, I remember," Jane said.

The three walked to the window, the glow of the proto-star renewing their memories. Henry turned to Timothy. The old man looked at him, tears in his eyes, reflecting the bright light of the birth star. "I know you," Henry said.

"Yes," Timothy answered, nodding.

"And you..." Henry said, turning toward Jane.

"I only just realized it," she said, looking at Henry. "I did not remember the cold and my death in the snow, nor did I before recall the wars of the future and my struggle to find truth from the past. Why did we live in such times of struggle?"

"It is what we chose," Timothy said. "I remember, and now we can choose to return or to be at peace. Peace at last."

Henry turned to face the window. "Peace at last," he said, smiling into the great light.

THE FIRST MARTIAN

It was the 40th sol of my stay on Mars. I took my eyes from the microscope lens and looked onto the hazy world outside. It had been nearly 30 hours since I had any rest, and my body was beginning to shake with fatigue. This so-called red wasteland was a treasure trove, and I was looking at its crown jewel. Life.

I discovered the microscopic extremophile in a chunk of broken permafrost, approximately 50 miles from my base in the Medusae Fossae Formation. I immediately reported the find to Mission Control and NASA was scheduled to make the announcement in two hours Earth time.

The microbes thrived on a plot of Martian land that had been sold for colonization. The little guys were swarming in a lump of freshly excavated ground. Construction on the new colony had been underway for months. Heavy machinery and a small collection of workers were long-term residents of the spot. The plan was to dig deep enough to create underground retreats where humans could live indefinitely and escape the effects of the radiation that penetrates the thin Martian atmosphere.

Trillionaires and billionaires staked their claim to the land years before I even imagined my visit to Mars. Every rich person alive was trying to get a piece of Martian real estate. It was an odd business. Mars wasn't a very nice place to vacation, and especially not to live. My guess was, they too wanted their names written in the scrolls of history as pioneers and innovators of the new frontier. They wanted Martian towns and states to bear their names; longed to become heroes in the new manifest destiny. I knew the eventual colonization spelled doom for the lifeform under my microscope. It seemed absurd to hope for a microbe's right to live unperturbed on its own planet. Even if I tried to be their champion and argue the fact that humans evolved from single-celled organisms and we could be changing the course of an entire planet's biological identity, I doubted the most important people on Earth would care about a few microbes they could easily assume never existed at all. Except I would prove that they did.

A buzz sounded from my monitor and I left the window. "Rory, you still up?" Commander Tabitha Clarke's voice was crisp and energetic over the speaker.

"Yes."

"Have you gotten any sleep?" she asked.

"A little."

"A drowsy teammate is a dangerous one," she said. Tabitha was always brimming with little aphorisms of apparent wisdom.

"I'm not tired," I lied.

"Just humor me and take a nap," she said. "Anyway, enforcing your bedtime was not why I wanted to talk to you. Can you take the rover out for a spin around 1300?"

"They're supposed to announce my find in two hours."

"I understand that and I'm sorry to cut your celebration short, but we need someone to check the W3 weather station again. Everyone else at your basecamp is busy. Patrick is running diagnostics on the air purity sensors and Marda is cleaning out and collecting samples of dust in the ducts. It would really help."

"It's malfunctioning again?" I asked.

"Yes, one of the sensors stopped working. There's a replacement for it in your storage area."

"I'll take care of it."

"Make sure you're sharp," Tabitha said. "There's been talk of a storm moving in tomorrow evening, but you know a Martian storm can be unpredictable. You need to be fresh."

The call light went dark and I knew she was right. I ambled to my bed. I set my alarm for two hours and pulled the covers over my fatigued form. The sheets smelled sterile and metallic, like everything on Mars. I missed the scents of Earth—the fresh air *and* the polluted air. I missed the colors green and blue. As I drifted into my first sleep in over a sol, the same vision that plagued my consciousness for five years appeared. I could never get far enough away to escape the image of her, those eyes that watered with superficial tears and those lips that mouthed an insincere apology. Only now she was surrounded by a tawny sky and a fierce wind turned her to dust. She haunted me. I saw her every night in my dreams. Her legacy followed me like a dark and uncertain storm. A clouded version of my past, which I never wanted to bring to light.

The loud ringing of the alarm pierced my slumber like an arrow through flesh. I jerked my head up and inspected the time. I'd overslept, pressed snooze, and no one had roused me. I only had a few hours to prepare the rover for my journey to the weather station. I lurched from my bed and went to my computer. My heart raced as I searched for a recording of the announcement of my discovery. There was no mention of Mars. No mention of life on Mars. And no mention of me. It was never announced.

I quickly dialed Tabitha's number. "Hello, Rory," she answered. "I was expecting a call from you."

"They didn't run it. They didn't mention my find."

"I know. I'm sorry."

"What are they waiting for? Why wasn't I notified?"

"I was supposed to tell you, but I thought it was best to let you rest. They decided it wasn't the right time to make the announcement. We still don't know a lot about the bacterium, and they think it would be better if we learned more before making a statement."

"What do you mean? I told them plenty." My face grew warm with rage, and I forced my knuckles into fists to keep my voice from bursting with anger. "They're like the psychrophile bacterial growth found in the permafrost of Siberia. They have slow biochemical reactions. They have proteins adapted to the cold and a thick membrane which enables them to survive higher levels of radiation. What more do they want?"

"Is it infectious?"

"It hasn't shown signs of being an infectious agent at all. For one, it wouldn't like the environment of a human body."

"Where do you think it came from?"

"Came from? Where do you think we came from?"

"Exactly." Tabitha paused a moment. "This announcement is going to raise a lot of questions, Rory. We need to be more prepared for the obvious ones and the not-so-obvious."

"What do you mean?

"Well, this will cause a lot of religious, philosophical, ethical, and scientific enquiries. People are going to question you. I believe you, Rory. However, your past doesn't necessarily help this discovery's legitimacy."

My breath caught in my chest. "Are you serious? You're saying you think I fabricated the find?"

"I don't think you did, but it was brought up as a possibility at the most recent meeting. No one else found a sample. You're the only one. You could have snuck an Earth bacterium on the space shuttle and kept it alive for this moment. Or it could have come from the equipment being used to dig the foundation of the colony and you spun it into something sensational. I'm not saying that's what you did, but your past and your mother—"

A flame of resentment spiked within me. "I'm not my mother," I answered bitterly.

"I know you aren't. But not everyone knows you like I do."

"Why would they let me be on this mission if they didn't trust me?"

"It came up when you applied. I made the call. You're a promising young scientist and what your mother did shouldn't ruin the benefits of having you on our team."

"You just didn't figure I'd find anything," I said.

"No one else has," Tabitha said. "We're sending a small team to check the site and to get a second evaluation. I'm sorry about all this. I'm sure they'll vindicate you."

I looked at the clock and let out an irritated sigh. "Who are you sending?"

"Gomez, Smith, and Peterson. They're planning to head out tomorrow morning from the Valles Marineris base and get there before the storm hits. They're taking the nitrojet, so they need to know live weather reports on the southeast side of Medusae Fossae to know when to shut off and deploy their chute. Are you prepared to take the rover out?"

"I was about to start preparing."

"Good," Tabitha said. "We've decided Marda is going to be joining you. I'm sorry about all this."

"I guess it can't be helped," I said, ending the call with my commander.

All the various checks for the rover were written in a large database. I went over them one by one, trying to focus my thoughts on the mission ahead. I loved taking the rover out. Driving a terrestrial vehicle reminded me of home. Only, everything else was vastly different.

It was the third time this weather station had malfunctioned in my 40-sol stay. Although I had been trained to fix every part of it and had fixed it once before, I was beginning to think it needed to be replaced altogether and that was a task I did not feel confident in accomplishing. There were always small glitches on Mars, but a full replacement would take weeks, months. Time that none of us had.

"Hello, Roar," Marda said as she entered the room. Her strawberry-blond hair was pulled back, and her uniform was clean and starched. I looked down at my own disheveled uniform and felt embarrassed. "How's the ol' Corvette looking?"

"Fine," I answered, kneeling down next to the rover to check the tire pressure. I wasn't always in the mood for Marda's personality; at times her sense of humor was a godsend and at others it was an annoyance.

"It's ridiculous that they don't believe you." Marda leaned in close as I knelt on the floor. "I might only be the rock jock here, but I can tell when someone's got a good head on their shoulders."

"So, I guess they decided I needed help changing out the sensor this time?"

"I guess so." Marda started packing the rover, methodically arranging the cargo. "I think everyone is worried about the weather. Besides, I like it better than staying here with Patrick."

"Sure," I said. I felt an irate tinge of contempt toward Marda. I finished my inspections and threw my luggage on top of Marda's neatly stacked bags.

"It's more than a three-hour drive to the station. Did you bring snacks in that bag?"

"Of course," I said.

"Good, I wasn't going to share."

"Are you two off to the weather station, then?" Patrick's astute British accent floated in from the back door of the rover. Patrick was the typical science nerd—meticulous about everything, including the facial hair displayed on his face. He probably used an X-acto knife and a ruler every morning on his perfectly shaped circle beard.

"Come to wish us off, then?" Marda asked in a rather good imitation of his accent.

"Wish I could go too. I've been feeling a bit stir-crazy. It might be nice to get out for a while," Patrick said, ignoring her inflected jab. "I'll try my best to keep track of your location." Patrick turned toward Marda and softened his expression. "Be safe. I'll see you in a few hours." It wasn't a mystery to anyone that Patrick had a thing for Marda. They were both unattached and worked in close proximity. I was convinced Marda didn't reciprocate Patrick's advances, but after being on Mars another 40 sol, she might come around to the idea. Marda could be a lovely person, but I wasn't on Mars for romance. Friendship is a must when you're one of about 15 humans on a planet, but romance could get messy.

131

We waited for Patrick to leave the garage and opened the door. A rush of dust and rock fragments blew in. The dust was a major problem whenever the doors opened. Marda released the break and we throttled forward. The familiar bumpy, uneven jolts of the Martian terrain rocked our necks as we escaped to the outside.

"Over six hours there and back," Marda said, concentrating on the terrain ahead.

Mars was an endless sea of dry red dirt that went on forever. Only the howl of the wind and the mysterious shifting of rock were audible. The wind alone seemed to come alive on Mars. It created. It destroyed. It shaped. It birthed colossal dust devils that danced across the barren land like ghosts trapped on a forgotten world. As I looked out the window of the rover, I could see a dust devil twirling in the distance, haunting and dangerous.

"I thought the winds were supposed to be fairly calm," Marda said, noting the dust devil.

"There was a downburst to the west. We should be clear of it."

"I hate seeing those things. They make me nervous."

I nodded and pulled up the feed from the weather station we were approaching. The station had no wind speed data. I cleared the feed and sat up in my seat, keeping an eye open for sharp rocks and crevices.

"So, they don't believe you found life because of something your mom did?" Marda asked.

I was surprised Marda brought it up. I looked away from the road and tightened my seatbelt. "Yeah, I guess," I said. The road rocked our bodies back and forth in an uncomfortable seated dance.

"Who was she?" she said. I gave Marda a glare. I wasn't there for a counseling session. I was there to change a damn sensor. "Oh, come on. I'm just trying to understand the situation. I want to be on your side. I know I'll still be on your side. You're a good guy, Rory. You're passionate about your work. You're not full of bullshit. You say what you mean, and I just want to be able to help you."

"She killed people," I answered bluntly.

"What?" Marda said.

"Dr. Doreen Holden."

"Oh." The conversation went silent. Only the crunching of rock and sand under the weight of the rover broke the lull. "I need to admit that I don't know who she is. I'm sorry. I mean, were you ever in danger? Did you know anyone—"

"It wasn't like that. She made a bogus drug and it got put on the market." I was used to spitting out the story. I hated talking about it, but it was better to just puke out the details so the subject could be dropped. "It was never tested and there were never any clinical trials. She made everything up. The drug could have been apple cider if she wanted it to be, but for some reason she made it lethal. A lot of powerful people believed in her and gave her money and support without understanding the science or fact-checking her. I think overall thirty people lost their lives, much more are living with health problems because of it. It was called Flobeta. It was supposed to cure early onset Alzheimer's."

"Flobeta. That was your mom?"

I nodded.

"I'm so sorry, Rory."

"I've learned to live with it," I said. "I was 15 years old at the time. A lot of people thought that was old enough to

133

know something about it, though. My mom was good at manipulating people and even better at keeping secrets."

"Where is your mom now?" Marda asked.

"She died." I looked out the window at the red dust devil in the distance and felt tired.

"Well, you've got my respect," Marda said. "You've got to be tougher than nails to make it this far with a story like that. If people hold that shit against you, they're wrong." Marda looked at me and smiled.

We arrived at the weather station thirty minutes later than anticipated. An unexpected headwind made it hard for the rover to keep pace. There was an ominous haze to the sky which made the area gloomy.

"Looks spooky out there," Marda said.

"There's been a drop in pressure. We better hurry and inspect this thing." I unbuckled and found my suit. Marda quickly followed my lead.

A gritty wind hit us as we exited the rover. "It's the wind speed sensor that's on the fritz," I said. The weather station was about 12 feet tall. The majority of the sensors were located near the top. I placed a foot on the ladder built onto the side of the station, holding the replacement part in my hand as I located the defective sensor. Marda held out the toolbox and I took a screwdriver from the box and began to climb. The faulty sensor had a thick layer of dust covering its surface and dirt weaved itself into the screw heads, making my work to free the sensor more difficult. I scraped the residue free, causing a small arc of static electricity.

"How's it looking?" Marda asked from the ground.

"Looks like we've got some dust sticking to the screw threads. My guess is dust got inside the sensor too. I bet we can reuse it if we clean it out. I'm going to replace it for now though."

"The damn dust. It gets everywhere," Marda said.

From 12 feet up, I could see a mass of red dust on the horizon. The wind picked up, throwing more sand and dust at my helmet as I worked. It continued to pelt the weather station as I tried to attach the new sensor in place. I placed the old, dusty sensor in my satchel and slung it over my shoulder, and then I adjusted and screwed the new sensor in place. "All done," I said, heading back down the ladder.

"All that work for a wind sensor," Marda said. A gust of wind made her veer off to one side. "I hope it works."

"I'll need to check that it does before we head out," I said, placing the screwdriver in the leg pocket of my space suit.

"Anything else need to be done before we leave?" Marda asked.

"There's an awful lot of dust covering the instruments and the solar panels," I replied.

"I'll clean them off while you check the wind sensor." Marda took a towel from her satchel and began climbing the ladder.

I quickly took out my computer pad and checked the weather station's readings. The wind was pounding my suit and making it nearly impossible to use the touch screen. "I may have to go in the rover to check this," I said. I flicked the touch screen once more and the readings finally appeared. All the sensors were working normally. The wind sensor was reading above normal wind gusts, which seemed accurate for what I was feeling on the ground. "Marda, we should get out of this wind—"

I heard a sharp pop and a thud and Marda was on the ground. "Marda!" I yelled. I ran to her and knelt beside her. Marda's eyes were closed. I nudged her shoulders to try and rouse her, but she was still. Hoisting her over my shoulders, I quickly took her into the rover. Once her helmet was off, I found a blackened puncture point in her suit near her neck. There was an intense burn on the left side of her neck and a smaller burn on her upper right breastbone marking the exit wound. She had no pulse. I quickly performed CPR, praying to whoever would listen. "Come on, Marda! Come on! You're going to make it!"

I sat in the rover with nothing but the thrashing of dust on the windows to break the silence. All communications had been knocked out by the dust storm and Marda was dead. I did my best to resuscitate her. I continued to try until her lips turned cold and firm and I collapsed from exhaustion. It was dark and I was alone. I sat with only dark thoughts for company. If it had taken me a few more minutes to change the sensor out, it would have been me instead of Marda. I tried to send several messages out. They failed to send. All my calls were dropped. There was nothing to do but wait out the howling darkness. It was far too dangerous to travel in a storm, especially at night. Marda's body rested in the back of the rover. I wrapped her up neatly in a blanket. I tried not to look back there. Occasionally, my eyes would stray toward her and I would think she moved. I talked to her every so often, but I knew she wasn't going to answer. Marda would never speak again.

Looking out the window was not a comfort. Much like the darkness of space, the darkness of the Martian night could overwhelm a person. It was enigmatic, filled with mysterious whispers and thuds. At times, it sounded like a beast scratched and clawed at the exterior of the rover. I knew it was dust and rock blowing against the vehicle, but the sounds were too troubling to keep rational thought intact. I wanted to turn the lights on, but I had to conserve the power. I layered myself with everything I could and placed my helmet back on and huddled into a ball in my space suit. I was freezing. The night before it had reached -64 degrees Celsius. I had enough power to turn the rover on for fifteen minutes every two hours, but I could only do it long enough each time to raise the temperature to -19. There was nothing to do but sleep. I closed my eyes, trying to dream myself away from the nightmare, but all I could see was Marda's face and the red devils made of dust.

I woke in the early hours of the morning. The storm lifted and I had to make the drive back quickly. I still couldn't contact Patrick or any of the other bases. I drove fast, in a delirious state of madness and fear. I didn't want to be alone anymore. I needed someone to commiserate with, but I also knew Patrick wasn't going to take the news of Marda's death well.

Dust devils coiled on the horizon as I pulled into base camp. My communications were still down. I found my helmet and locked it into place. I stepped out into the harsh Martian air once more to alert Patrick that I had to open the rover storage door. I pressed the call button on the payload door and waited. My stomach twisted into knots.

"You were gone long enough," Patrick's voice echoed over the speaker.

"Can you let me in, Patrick? Communications are down. And…we need to talk in the conference room."

"Okay, I'll see you two there," he answered. I looked up to the heavens. The tawny sky was turning red. Another storm was coming.

I waited for Patrick in the conference room, delirious and drained of most thought. I had gone straight there without taking my suit off. I sat in the sterile room, red dust and debris falling from my suit onto the clean white floor.

"Hey," Patrick said as he entered the room. "Why are you still in your suit? You're bringing all sorts of stuff in, Rory. It's against protocol. Where's Marda?"

"Something happened when we were checking the weather station."

"Where's Marda?" he asked again, his voice growing urgent.

I cleared my throat and hoarsely began to explain. "She climbed the weather station. She was cleaning it and something happened. Some electrical charge or dry lightning from the incoming dust storm. I'm not sure—"

"Where is she?"

"She's gone, Patrick. She got hit by an electrical arc and I couldn't save her."

"That's not possible."

"I'm so sorry. I couldn't save her. I tried. She wouldn't come back. She—"

"That's not possible!" Patrick shouted.

"Patrick…"

"You're lying!" Patrick left the room. I followed.

He charged through the hall, turning in the direction of the rover storage area. I slowed and followed at a distance. Patrick's sobs echoed off the walls as I reached the entrance to the garage. The back hatch of the rover was open and Patrick sat inside, cradling Marda's body in his arms. I approached quietly. Patrick rocked back and forth, mumbling compliments into her deaf ears. His hands petting her hips and neck as he spoke. I wanted to shake him and make him stop. I didn't feel Marda would have been comfortable with such a strong show of affection. She had often rolled her eyes at his faintly veiled admirations, and occasionally even left the room when he would appear in the kitchen for his meals. It never worried me before. Seeing him hold her dead body in such a way made me wish I had said something to end the behavior while she was still alive. Patrick pressed his lips to Marda's, and a feeling of sickness overcame me.

"That's enough, Patrick."

"What did you do to her!" Patrick pushed Marda's body aside and jumped toward me. My back hit the wall. Even in my suit, the force took my breath away. My attacker's eyes were red and wild. "Out all night and she ends up dead. You're a damn liar."

My face stung from the impact of Patrick's fist and I fell to the floor. "I didn't do anything to her! It was an accident! It was a terrible accident!" Pain seared through my abdomen as he began kicking it over and over and over. "Stop," I gasped. "I didn't do anything to her." I felt the warm, sludgy fluid of my own blood drip from the corners of my mouth.

"You've always been a little creep! Watching me and watching her!" Patrick grabbed me by the neck ring of my suit and dragged me to the hall. "I told them I never wanted you to come. You can't trust someone with a murderer for a mother." My arms slapped at Patrick, but he was strong, and I was weak from a night of exhaustion and cold.

I saw the door and the red Martian sky through its thick glass window. Patrick stopped at it. "Why did you do this, Rory?" Patrick twisted his grip on my suit and pulled me close to face him. He firmly grasped my short hair between his fingers and pulled my head back. I cried out in pain, my scalp stinging from his action. "Was it because of your microbes? Everyone knows you brought them. You know, after I'm finished here, I'm going to kill every last one of them, and if for some godforsaken reason they really are where you say they are, I'll go out there and I'll sanitize the situation. I'll kill them all off. You won't be remembered." The pain made me delirious and reality blurred. "I'm going to kick you outside now," Patrick said, his grip so tight on my hair I was certain he would rip it from my scalp.

"No, please," I begged, searching with my hands for a helmet. My mind was a blur of fear and fight, then I realized I still had the screwdriver in the front leg pocket of my suit. I reached for it as Patrick dialed the code for the door. I pulled it from my pocket. A scream escaped my throat as I shifted all my weight and jammed the tool into my assailant's neck. The pain on my scalp relaxed, my head fell, and everything was black.

The smell of iron woke me. I opened my eyes. A red sticky mess surrounded me. I lifted myself off the floor, and Patrick's lifeless body came into full view. An unspeakable amount of blood surrounded his face and neck. I found the screwdriver in a bloody pool next to me. I must have pulled it from Patrick's neck when he released his hold and I collapsed to the floor. Despair came over me. As I examined the mess that surrounded me, I began to cry.

"Oh my god," a voice gasped. The sound was so foreign and out of place that I hardly reacted. A slender woman ran from the scene, soon returning with two others. It was Gomez, Smith, and Peterson. They had gotten through the storm to access my find.

It was a seven-month journey back to Earth. I was locked in my room. The living quarters on the ship were small. I was allowed to participate in routine tasks, exercise, and eat, but never alone. I was the first prisoner on a space mission. The first suspected murderer on Mars.

"It comes on in 30 seconds, Rory," Commander Tabitha Clarke said, taking a seat next to me. After everything, another team was sent to inspect the microbes. They found them exactly where I had initially discovered them.

The screen flickered on and a reporter appeared in front of the Kennedy Space Center. "Today NASA has made it official. There is life on Mars. Tiny microbes able to withstand the extreme climate of Mars have been found. But I'm afraid there is a darker and more disturbing side to the story. Earlier today, it was leaked that Dr. Rory Holden, son of the infamous Flobeta inventor, and the scientist who is said to have made the initial discovery of the life, is due to be questioned in the deaths of two of his colleagues who worked at the base in the Medusae Fossae Formation alongside him. If convicted, Dr. Holden will be the first human to commit murder on Mars. Nothing has been confirmed, but we will be sure to keep you up to date on the facts and disturbing new details."

Tabitha turned the screen off. "I'm so sorry, Rory. You don't deserve this." She placed a hand on my shoulder a moment and left me.

I knew even if my innocence was proven and self-defense was recognized, the killing of a colleague would be my legacy. People would say I was nothing more than the product of a mad woman, whose murderous tendencies were passed down. The story of the life I found would forever be tainted with death and murder.

IN
MEMORIAM
MACHINE

Charley opened his eyes. Greeting him was the same old, worn tile ceiling. Hushed and workaday voices came to him through muffled ears. The occasional yelp of a sneaker treading over-polished floor made its way to his damaged cochlea. Lifting the covers from his chin he examined his hands—liver spotted and wrinkled. Charley couldn't guess what they used to look like. Memory was only in the now. He could no longer recall his past. It was taken from him by time and decay. He was old and probably not long for the world. He tried to focus, to remember, but everything just floated away in a haze. A morning sunbeam cut through his bedroom window. Specs of dust caught in its ray remained in chaotic suspension as if not knowing where they belonged. He thought it reminded him of something. It was a memory he was on the cusp of remembering but could never quite reach.

"Good morning, Charley."

Charley turned to see a woman enter his room. "Morning, Krissy," he answered. "It is Krissy?"

"Yes, very good Charley," said Krissy. "Are you feeling alright this morning?" Her young eyes filled with concern. She had a lovely face. Long, dark locks outlined her delicate features, and she gave off an aura of calm that Charley quite enjoyed.

"I don't know, you tell me."

"Well, only you know that, Charley."

"I don't seem to know who I am."

The woman's brow furrowed. "Do you want to use your machine again today?"

"Machine? What machine?"

"You don't remember?" Krissy stepped close, leaning down toward Charley. She pressed her palm to his head and gave a sad smile. Her touch was cold and firm, yet Charley found comfort in it.

"I'm sorry." Krissy took a seat on Charley's bed. "Are…are we friends?" he asked.

The woman laughed with a kindness that made Charley feel drawn to her. "I like to think we are friends most days. You remember my name, but do you know what I do here?"

"I…I believe you take care of me. I'm too old to do much and you help me." The shaky and elderly tone of his own voice made Charley depressed. The woman sitting next to him was so young and vital. She had her entire life before her, and he couldn't even recall his own. The life he had lived could have been worthless for all he knew.

"You are correct. I watch over you and others here. Do you remember where you are?"

Charley let out a sigh and sat back in his pillows, "Unfortunately, yes. I am in a nursing home."

"Are you unhappy, Charley?"

"Very," he said, slumping deeper into his pillows.

"Why is that?"

"Because I can't remember a thing. I don't know who I am. I don't know my life. I…I remember I am Charley, you are Krissy, this is my room, and out there I get my meals, but beyond that it's empty."

"Last week you didn't remember your name and you didn't know mine," she said, smiling. "You are making progress."

"Can you cure old?" he asked sarcastically.

"It takes time to tap back into your memories. Here, take your medicine. It'll help," Krissy took a small container from her pocket and opened the lid for Charley to take.

Charley examined the pills in his palm and slapped them into his mouth. Krissy handed him a glass of water and he swallowed hard.

"If I told you I could show you your life, would you want to see it?"

"Show me? Of course I would want to see it."

"I think we can bump your time up to an hour today." Krissy got up from the bed and walked over toward the far wall. She typed a code into a large screen on the wall. 675441. Charley knew he would soon forget the path her fingers took around the pad, but nevertheless he couldn't help but try and repeat the numbers into memory. He had a sudden suspicion that he liked numbers but he didn't know why. A small opening widened as if a mouth had opened in the wall and Krissy took a small metallic square from within. The mouth in the wall closed. She pressed a button on the mysterious curved metal square and three spider-like arms ejected from three sides.

"Is that the machine?" Charley asked, inspecting the thing with suspicion.

"Yes," Krissy said, bringing it closer for his inspection. "It helps you remember things. It contacts the area of your brain where your memories are hidden, the places you have a hard time accessing now, and helps you remember."

"So, I could remember my 13th birthday if I wished?"

Krissy smiled, "Yes, Charley you could, but recently you've been interested in a different time in your life. Does that sound familiar?"

149

Charley looked down and forced his mind to search for the answer, then he remembered. It came to him quite unexpectedly, as if a wave had propelled the thought to him and it would float back out to sea if he didn't speak it. "The war," he said. "I asked and you told me I could visit any time I had a mind to. That was only yesterday, but I don't remember using this." He looked at the device again.

Krissy looked at him with excitement. "You're starting to remember things."

"Then why don't I remember using this machine?"

"I think you do," Krissy paused a moment as if accessing some information out of reach. "You visited your 13th birthday and you made a wish. Do you remember what the wish was?"

"I..." Charley began to laugh with recollection, as if he were only just there. "I think I wished for a dog."

"See, you do remember."

"Yes, I remember a little now."

"If you visit a memory of the war, I am afraid it won't make you happy. I've warned you several times."

"But I need to know. I don't remember my life, Krissy. I want to remember the good and the bad."

"Okay, Charley, but if it does not make you happy or help with your memory, I cannot do it for you any longer."

"Remembering the truth about my life is what will make me happy."

Krissy's face grew grave. "That is not always the case. Not everyone's memories are pleasant."

"So? It's their life. I have a right to know my own life."

Krissy bent down with the memory machine and slowly rested it upon Charley's temple. The three small spider legs

150

latched on and injected themselves into Charley's skull. He jumped from the unexpected sensation. It didn't hurt, but it felt as though he had invited something foreign inside. He had not expected something so invasive. He felt a bead of sweat fall down his face and realized he could not control his breath. He was on the verge of screaming out in protest when the room transformed around him.

The sound of waves crashed against a shore. Charley saw white, blinding sunlight. He blinked until his new world came into view. He was on a beach. The sky above was blue and cheerful. The fine granular beads of warm sand under him gave him a renewed feeling of calm. He took some grains in his hands. His hands were young and clear.

"Charley," a man's voice called out. "Hey dipshit, it's time to get a move on it."

Charley sat up to see a group of soldiers surrounding him. "Dillion," he said. "Dillion Walton?"

"Yeah, numb nuts," Dillion replied. "Captain's ordered us to move up the line. You must be wiped out. Come on, I'll help you up." Dillion offered Charley his hand and was hoisted up by his comrade.

"Thank you," Charley said.

"Man, that accent," Dillion said with a now familiar look of friendship on his face. "Where did you say you were from, Charley?"

"No place special," Charley answered.

"Ha, not special," Dillion scoffed. "I figure everywhere is special in these times." He looked at Charley with an understanding sadness in his eyes. "Anyone special? Come on, we're moving up. The least you can do is finally tell me something, anything about yourself."

.A. Hogan

Charley thought. Something was there. A memory he hadn't been able to access. Something important. Someone substantial to him. "Yes," he answered. "A daughter. I was drafted and she signed up willingly right before I had to leave."

"She sounds brave," said Dillion.

"She..." A memory of a young girl climbing a tree suddenly came to him. Amber sunlight filtered through autumn leaves and the girl was reaching for a kite within the tree's branches. With one arm she grasped a branch and with the other she reached for the kite. Standing on a thick limb, she went to her tiptoes. She reached and reached. "She is very brave. Takes after her mother and not me," he found himself answering. Her mother. Charley searched for a memory but was unable to recall who this person had been.

"Well, then I wish her mother was here instead of you," Dillion said, laughing.

"She died," Charley answered.

"Oh, I'm sorry. I didn't know—"

"Do you have family?" Charley said with enough determination to turn the line of questioning away from himself.

"I do. There are seven of us. One beautiful wife, three ornery kids, and two scruffy hound dogs. When I get back, I promised them a tree house. That is, if my wife hasn't already made it without me. She likes to be outside almost as much as the hound dogs."

"Sounds nice," Charley said.

"How old is your daughter?"

"She just turned twenty."

"Twenty. You must have started young."

52

"I was only seventeen when she was born. Your kids, how old are they?"

"Oh, they're still young. The youngest is five and the oldest is only nine. Where's your daughter stationed?"

"I haven't been told."

"They like to keep us out of the loop, don't they? Just try and put the blame on the New Nation."

"Yeah, damn New Nation."

Charley heard a whiz and a pop. "N.N. on the south cliff!" a voice yelled, followed by a thunderous boom. Charley felt his feet leave the sand and he was thrown toward the ocean with a collection of debris and dust. He hit the water and a rush of liquid surrounded him. Salt water rushed into his mouth and nose, and he coughed for breath. He emerged to hear muffled echoes of surf and screams. Something softly bumped his side and he turned to see Dillion floating beside him. "Dillion!" he called out, clutching at him.

"Move! Move!" someone commanded. Someone else grabbed his jacket and lifted him away. He stumbled to find his footing, watching Dillion's body float slowly back and forth with the surf. Sunlight reflected off the water, obscuring everything in burning light. Large lingering debris and dust were the only things to break up the glare.

Charley sat at the table in the dining room. Other old and unsatisfied humans sat around him, nudging their mush with spoons. He looked at the clock. It was 12:45. Krissy had promised him more time with the machine at 1:00.

Since his last visit into his past, he could hardly wait to get back to it. The war was dark and miserable, but so was his shut-in life at the nursing home. There was nothing to fight for in the present. He was only waiting for time to stop ticking. He longed to remember his daughter. He wanted to remember her name. Her face. Her story. He wanted her to come and visit him. He had asked Krissy if she could call his daughter for him, but she was called away suddenly by an emergency and he hadn't seen her since.

"It's time to go back to your room," an attendant said.

"Yes, thank you," Charley said, pushing his plate away. The attendant began rolling Charley's wheelchair from the dining room. "Do you think you could help me call my daughter?"

"I'd love to help, Charley. But you know I only move you guys around. I'll find Krissy and ask her to try for you."

"Thanks," Charley said, disappointed. He longed to hear from his daughter. He could recall almost nothing of her, but he knew he felt love for her and was certain that she loved him. She was all Charley had. He could feel that there had been a void in their lives when her mother died, and they had tried their best to fill it with their own admiration and love for each other. He was certain she would want to talk to him, and he longed to know if he had any grandchildren. "Please, do ask Krissy. I would love to hear from my daughter. I...I can't remember her name." The attendant lifted Charley into his bed and adjusted the blankets around him. "I miss being able to walk on my own," Charley lamented.

"Well, if you could do that I'd be out of a job," the attendant said.

"You're a nice young man. I wish I could remember your name."

"Well, thank you. I'll just go get Krissy and see what she can do about getting ahold of your daughter."

Charley leaned back into his pillows and focused. He could feel the dry skin on his forehead wrinkle and flake as he tried to recall his own daughter's name. He huffed and squinted and searched for the name, but it was no use. "What is my daughter's name?" he said to the walls.

Krissy entered and saw him in his despondent state. "Is everything alright?"

"I want to speak to my daughter."

"Of course," Krissy said. "Official call days are usually on Saturdays. Do you think you could wait until then?"

"Well, uh—" Charley struggled to find composure. He was so frustrated he could scream. "What's today?"

"It's Tuesday."

"Oh," he huffed. "Do I have to wait? I really need to speak to her."

"I am sorry," Krissy said. She placed her soft hand on his and looked at him regretfully. "Maybe the machine would help. We could start a little early. What do you say, Charley?"

Charley agreed and Krissy typed in the code and received the memory machine from the wall. "I have it set so that it will take you wherever you wish to go."

"But, I can't remember where to go," Charley said.

"You will." Krissy pressed the machine to his temple and the arms pierced through to his mind once more.

Charley saw green grass covered in debris. Stuffed toys, some gutted, others whole. Clothes spread across the lawn. An empty dog bowl. He leaned down to examine the bowl. The name Rex had been painted across the bottom. He wondered where Rex was now. He studied the scattered innards of Rex's family's home and let out a sigh.

He looked up from the empty dog bowl and tattered belongings of the unknown, missing family and saw houses upon houses destroyed and collapsing. His fellow soldiers walked the wasted suburban street toward more destruction.

"I visited this area before the war," a soldier said, stopping next to Charley. She coughed and took a bite of some of her rations. "Families. People just trying to live out their lives and the N.N. has to come in and pulverize them. Rachel Hill." The woman nodded in greeting.

"Charley Oakley." He nodded in return. "Rachel…" Charley searched for what he wanted to say. "Rachel, that's my daughter's name."

"And where is she?"

"I…don't know."

"Incoming!" a voice yelled.

Charley felt a biting pain in his ear and neck. The world blurred and faded in and out. He felt a soft touch across his chest. "I've got you, Charley!" Rachel yelled. "I've got you…I've…" the voice faded and changed, growing younger and less urgent. "I've got it, Daddy!" his daughter's voice came to him.

His daughter, Rachel, ran toward him, a yellow and blue kite trailing behind her. "I've got it, Daddy!" she said excitedly. "Mommy, come look!" Charley swung his head around, searching. *Where is Mommy? Who is Mommy?*

Rachel ran past. Charley followed, rounding a large tree in the yard. There was a woman sitting on the ground, planting flowers. Her back was turned and Rachel ran up to her.

"You got it! Oh, my brave little girl," the woman said, turning to kiss her daughter. The face, Charley didn't recognize the face. She was beautiful and healthy and he knew that he loved her.

"Daddy was there to make sure I didn't fall," Rachel admitted.

"Oh, he was," the woman said, turning toward Charley. "I know he would have caught you." The woman's eyes met his, and a sudden warmth overwhelmed him. *This is my family. My home.*

"Charley, wake up! Wake up!" Charley found himself back on the street, searing pain in his ear. "Medic! I need a medic," Rachel Hill yelled. The ground vibrated underneath him. Charley watched Rachel's eyes search the streets. "Shit, we're going to have to run. Can you walk?" It hurt, but he could. Rachel flung Charley's arm around her shoulder and they struggled down the road. Fresh bodies and pulverized debris littered the streets, making it hard for them to advance.

A violent wind blew them to the ground and a voice like thunder yelled over a loudspeaker, "Stop where you are! Or you will be shot!"

A strong wind from a helicopter forced them to stay down. Charley turned to look at Rachel and found she was already looking at him. "Well, this is it, Charley," she said sadly.

Charley sat looking out the window. His memory of the past was becoming much clearer. He could picture his life with his daughter when she was young. He knew it had to have been pleasant. Something worth fighting for. She was worth fighting for. The New Nation wanted nothing but to destroy their way of life for a new autocratic, xenophobic, and anti-technological way. A bird landed on the window outside and Charley found himself wishing that he could fly. Fly to his daughter. Fly far from this prison of a nursing home. He would never know freedom again. He wondered what he had done after the war. Had Rachel stayed nearby? Did he remarry? Did they beat the New Nation in the end? There were so many things he still couldn't remember, but he knew it was coming back. Things were slowly resurfacing with every use of the machine, little pieces of the puzzle of his life were beginning to find a place in his mind. The bird outside his window flew away and footsteps entered his room.

"Good morning, Charley," Krissy said cheerfully. "Here are your morning pills. Now be sure to take all of them." Krissy handed him a handful of multicolored pills and a cup of water. Charley spread the collection out on his palm for inspection.

"Boy," he said. "I must be sick. Seems like more pills than yesterday."

"It comes with the territory."

"The territory?" he said, looking up at Krissy. "Oh, of being old. Yes, I see." Charley planted his palm to his mouth and swallowed the pills.

"Very good," she said. "Would you like to do an activity today? There's a pianist coming at two o'clock, and there's painting in the lobby in ten minutes."

"No!" he said with a panic he didn't understand. Krissy looked at him with concern.

"Are you alright?"

"Yes...Yes, I am sorry," he said. "I think I would just very much like to use the machine again today."

"Oh, I don't know Charley. That would be three days in a row. Don't you think you should rest?"

"Please," Charley begged. "I want to see my daughter again. Why does it keep taking me to the war? Why can't I just see my daughter?"

"The machine takes you to the memories your subconscious chooses."

"But I know every core of my being wants to see my daughter."

Krissy smiled. "Then it should let you see a memory of her. But not today. You need your rest."

"Then let me call her?"

"I'll see what I can do," Krissy assured him.

Charley sat in his room for what seemed like hours. The bird never returned to his window after Krissy left and he received no word on the call to his daughter. Charley gazed at the wall which held his machine. "I could make it," he said. After taking a few moments to formulate a plan, Charley decided he could reach the wall if he used his bed to help brace himself. He only needed to remember the code.

Charley focused. He thought long and hard, trying to recall the code Krissy had typed that opened the mouth in the wall. He recalled a 6, but what was to follow? There had been double 4s but in what order did they come? Suddenly, like a flash of light he remembered: 675441. He crept from his place on the bed. His arms and legs shaky and weak. "It's not far," he whispered, biting down on his lip. "It's not…far." His foot slid forward awkwardly. He gripped tightly to the sheets on his bed, slowly inching his way closer to the wall. Finally, he made it. He smacked the wall and a screen appeared. He slowly typed in the code and the machine presented itself. He released both hands from the bed. With an unsteady posture, he brought the machine to his temple, and with a sudden bolt the arms of the machine ejected and fastened themselves to his head.

Charley found himself walking toward a fence lined with barbed wire. The sky was gray and the grass brittle and lifeless. A cold air bit at his cheeks as he walked. His wrists stung. He looked down to see them tied tightly with steel wire. Rachel Hill walked on his right. It was clear that they had been walking like this for some time. He felt miserable and his feet hurt. Rachel looked as though she hadn't slept for days. Mud splattered across her vacant and emotionless face. Her expression reminded him of something. He searched his mind. It was an accident. An event in his life which he could feel was buried deep in the cracks of his memory. He pictured a small car. Pounded into a thin scrap of metal. Wedged between a tree and a large truck. Caution tape was strung about the scene of the vehicles and they were still pulling something from the wreckage, but he couldn't see what. A man paced beside the wreck. "I didn't see her. I didn't see her," he repeated to himself in a daze.

Charley continued past the scene toward an ambulance. He realized he wasn't walking there on his own, but there was a man supporting him by his arm and guiding him toward the ambulance. He knew the area. He knew the trees. It wasn't far from his home. Only a few blocks. But where was he being led? There was a gurney inside the ambulance. A white sheet resting over a lump which only made up half the bed. He approached and was helped inside where he took a seat. "Is this your wife, sir?" a man asked somberly, slowly removing the sheet. A woman's vacant face stared up. A flurry of memories came to him. Their wedding, the birth of Rachel, Christmases and summers spent hiking—a life of love and teamwork.

"Dad!" Charley turned to see his daughter staring toward them outside the ambulance. Terror spread over her face.

Charley felt a sudden sting in his back. "Keep moving," a man commanded, sticking the butt of a rifle on the small of Charley's back.

He quickened his pace. "Where do you think we are?" he asked Rachel Hill.

"Nowhere good," she replied, never looking at him.

"You!" a man yelled. "Be quiet!"

Charley began examining the area. There were trees lining the fence with tattered bags attached to their trunks. He squinted to make out what purpose the bags held and realized they weren't bags at all. They were people bound to the trunks. Prisoners like him and Rachel. As they grew closer, he could tell that many of the people were dead and the few who weren't were nearly there. New Nation soldiers poked and prodded him and Rachel through a gate, and it shut behind them with a blood-curdling screech.

"Watch them while I go get Commander Miller," a soldier told two others. Rachel Hill stood silently next to him. The look in her eyes told him that she was ready for death. His knees became weak and shaky and he fell to the ground. "Get up!" a voice commanded.

Charley struggled to stand but could not regain a footing with his arms tied. A pair of shiny boots paused in front of him and Charley forced his gaze up. A middle-aged man with slicked-back hair and a despotic twinkle in his eye looked down at him. "Stand him up," he commanded. Violent arms lifted him from the ground, and he wobbled onto his feet. "I am Commander Miller," the man said, looking from Charley to Rachel Hill. "I am in charge of this camp and I will be the sole and only person in charge of your fate for the remainder of your miserable lives." He looked toward Charley again and gave a sideways smile. Charley studied his face. It was a horrible face filled with fear that had morphed into indescribable hatred. He knew he would never be able to forget the monstrous look in the man's eyes. "So, who are they?" Commander Miller asked.

A soldier approached and handed him Charley and Rachel Hill's ID cards. "Hmm, okay, nobody special. Wait— Oakley. Didn't we have someone with this same last name once?" The men looked at him blankly. "Oh, I remember. It was a young lady. How do you all not remember? And more interesting, I think she had the same name as this one." The man pointed a boot toward Rachel Hill.

"Rachel," Charley gasped.

"Oh, do you know her?"

"My daughter. Where is she?"

"What are the odds?" Commander Miller laughed. "Well, I was going to just shoot you both, but now with this turn of events, I think I have something else in mind for you." Commander Miller's eyes met Charley's—they cut through him with their icy blue malice. Commander Miller drew his weapon and fired a shot. Charley heard a thud. He turned from Commander Miller's gaze to see Rachel Hill dead.

The view under his bed was just as he had imagined it—spotless and barren of anything interesting. His consciousness had released him from the memory machine after the painful recollections he had been shown, and he had since been stuck to the floor in his room at the nursing home.

"Charley!" Krissy ran to his side. "What happened?"

"I…I fell," he answered.

"Here, let me help you." Krissy lifted his frail form off the ground. Charley put all the strength he had into his legs. He never imagined he'd be so weak. Between the two of them they finally managed to rest him on the bed. Charley's breath grew heavy and deep. "Why in the world did you try and get your machine without me?"

"I…I had to see her," he panted. "I have to see my daughter."

A flicker of pity flashed in Krissy's eyes. She looked away and left him to fetch the machine off the floor. When she returned to face him, her face was pleasant and unassuming again. "That was very dangerous for you, you know."

"Well, did I die?"

"No, no you didn't," Krissy paused. "You must be more careful," she added with a smile. "If you wanted to use this so badly, I would have gotten it for you."

"Then why didn't you?" he demanded. "I asked and asked."

"Are you angry with me?"

"Yes! Of course, I am," he scoffed. "You leave me alone for an eternity and you never call my Rachel! The least you could do is let me find out what happened to her." Charley's voice cracked and he rested his head in his hands. "She died. Didn't she? That man…Commander Miller. He killed her." Tears readily flowed and he couldn't stop them though he tried. "He killed so many people."

Krissy's eyes grew wide and she stepped away. She stood in silence a few moments, unblinking. "Rachel Oakley isn't dead," she began. "If you really want to know the truth, it'll take time."

"She isn't dead?" Charley lifted his head. It was as if his whole world was evaporating into the past. "Why did you let me believe my daughter was dead?"

"You need to find out the truth for yourself. I should not step in and present the truth to you," she said.

"But my daughter is alive," he said. "Why can't I see her?"

"It's complicated," Krissy said.

"It's not complicated at all."

"Perhaps we should increase your time on the machine. It might be able to finish its work sooner than we thought,"

Krissy said, looking away as though she spoke to someone else.

"I just want answers," Charley said.

"Then we will try and answer them," Krissy replied, placing the machine to his temple. Pain shot through his head and before he could cry out he was once again in a memory.

An open stretch of road lay out before him. The hum of the road soothed him as he sat in silence watching the car drive itself to their destination. He spotted fishing poles and blankets in the back in the rearview mirror. He looked over at his daughter. Her phone sat unused beside her and she glared out the window. She was only about twelve, still not a woman. He tried to imagine what she looked like grown but couldn't recall. "What's wrong?" he asked.

"Where do you think the man that killed Mom is now?" she asked coldly.

"I don't know," Charley said. "I try not to think about it."

"I hate him," she said. "I wish he was dead and not her. I wish he had died before he was able to kill Mom. I wish I could have taken him out myself then she could be on this camping trip with us."

Charley's breath caught in his throat. "Rachel, don't say things like that. It was an accident. Yes, the man wasn't using a safe, self-driving car, and it was entirely human error on his part, but he didn't mean to do it. I'm sure it is something he struggles with every day."

"I hope he does," she scoffed. "I hope it eats him up inside."

"Rachel, I think you're letting it eat you up inside. You can't harbor hate and revenge like this. It'll turn you into

165

something you're not. Your mom wouldn't want that. She would say to forgive the man, think of her fondly, and live the best we can. Let go of this anger, honey. Let go of it."

Rachel turned toward her dad. "I'm sorry, Dad," she sobbed, reaching to embrace him. He held her close, soaking in her warmth.

A bitter wind stabbed at his face and he found himself back at war. Charley recalled Commander Miller standing before him as three other men bound him to one of the many trees encircling the camp. He wiggled and tested the binding. It was secure. "You don't want to pass out too long. You'll never wake," a voice said. Charley leaned his head to one side to look over at the tree next to him.

"How long have you been like this?" Charley asked.

"I can't remember," the man answered.

"Will they let us go?"

The man spit and gurgled as if trying to summon the strength for words. "Once you find yourself here, this is where you stay."

Panic took hold of Charley. He began struggling with his binding. He grunted and groaned and yelled out in rage. He tossed his head back and forth in an effort to gain momentum and caught sight of the tree to his left. A man, flesh peeling from muscle, lips missing, presenting a nasty snarl to the world, was hunched over, dead.

"He was alive the first day I was here. Don't remember his name," the man on Charley's right said, his voice becoming slurred and faint. "We become the trees. We become trees." Charley looked over to see the man had passed out. Charley's heart banged in his chest; he was certain the pounding was making the branches above him rattle and sway. He hadn't felt this helpless since his daughter Rachel left to volunteer for the war. He recalled her reasoning. Her desire to fight against the New Nation's oppression and ignorance. But he couldn't recall the shape of her face, the color of her eyes. The way she looked as a young woman, willingly leaving the safety of home for war. It was commonplace only a year before to send your child off to explore and learn in college, but there were only a few colleges left and little to safely explore. Children and parents alike were dealing with the uncertainty of civil war. He never gave his blessing, but he wasn't able to stop her.

The tree Charley was tied to shook from its roots. The man beside him groaned something Charley couldn't quite make out. "We're saff," the man said.

"What?" Charley asked. The rumble of planes had started in the distance and soon Charley could see the gray planes marked with red, white, and blue approaching from the west.

"We're saved!" the man beside him yelled.

Charley turned his head to see New Nation soldiers in the camp rushing to their vehicles. In the distance he could see Commander Miller walking with confidence toward a truck. A soldier held the door open for him to enter. Charley thought he saw a grin spread across the commander's face as he took out a small device from his pocket. Charley knew it was a detonator meant to destroy the camp and prisoners they were leaving behind. Commander Miller entered the vehicle and the truck sped off. Charley felt a heat growing behind him. A fiery orange glow bloomed and the shadow of his tree danced on the ground in front of him.

An alarm sounded, waking Charley from sleep. The same old, worn tile ceiling looked down on him from his bed in the nursing home. The machine was resting on the nightstand beside him. Charley sat up, realizing his muscles did not ache. He lifted himself from the bed with ease and felt good enough to venture toward the bathroom on his own. He felt renewed and his heart surged with a strange energy. The light flickered on in the bathroom and he approached the sink to rinse his face. He turned the water on and cupped the cool liquid in his hands. His hands weren't wrinkled. Nor did they have the spots of age and decay he had grown accustomed to. Charley looked to the mirror. He jumped back in horror and disbelief. He closed his eyes tightly and shook his head to rid himself of the nightmare in the reflection. He opened them again to see the image in the mirror had not changed. It was Commander Miller staring back at him. Charley placed his hands to his face, examining the hateful brow, the icy, blue eyes, and the snarled upper lip. It was hideous to look upon. He must have fallen into a horrible dream. A dream where his enemy had taken over his body. How had he arrived at this horrible and twisted reality? "No! This isn't real! This can't be real!" he shrieked.

Suddenly, strong arms grabbed hold of his flailing limbs. "Calm down," an orderly said, forcing Charley's arms still.

"What is happening? I've gone mad. I am not the man in that mirror! Please, call my daughter. Please, I need Rachel!"

"You don't have a daughter, Commander Miller," the orderly said.

Charley struggled for words. "Don't call me that. My name is Charley. My name is Charley Oakley. I need to speak to my daughter."

"Like I said, you don't have one." The orderly held him down across the bed while another began to tie his arms to the rails. "Do we give him his meds?" the orderly asked the other.

"They said not to today," the other replied.

"What are you doing?" Charley demanded.

"Just relax, Commander Miller."

"Stop calling me by that name. My name is Charley!"

The orderly smirked at the other and they grabbed Charley's arms. "We better call them. I think it's worked this time."

"This is amazing," the other replied excitedly.

"No!" Charley screeched and knocked one of the men to the floor and bolted for the door. He was surprised by his strength and speed. He rounded the hall and spotted Krissy.

"Oh, thank god, Krissy. You've got to help. I don't understand what's happening. I just, I just need to get out of here." Krissy looked past him, and Charley followed her gaze. Four burly men approached from behind. He shoved past Krissy and found a door. There was a stairwell behind it and Charley began climbing. "I'm not who they say. I…I can't be." He fought his way up the stairs and soon heard footsteps racing after him. "I'm not who you say!" he yelled. "You'll see. My daughter will come and she'll put things right." He found a door. The scent of fresh air met him through the exit. He circled the area. "Nowhere. Nowhere to go," he panted as he inspected the roof for an exit. Men appeared through the door. "Get back!"

"Calm down, Commander, let us take you back to your room and everything will be okay. You're not quite done with your treatment."

"Stop calling me that! My name is Charley Oakley. I was married. I had a family. My daughter's name is Rachel." Charley's knees began to shake. He ran his hands through his hair. A fingertip caught on a foreign lump. It was a large and circular hole on his temple. It was smooth and hard like metal. He held his hands up to his face. They were young and strong. "I…I don't understand." He looked over the edge. The city below was foreign and unknown. The way down was far. Charley turned back to see Krissy had joined the ranks of men.

"Don't let him jump!" she commanded. "Dart him! Now, before he gets too close to the edge!"

The world spun and Charley panicked. He locked eyes with Krissy and confusion pierced through his memories. "Rachel!" he yelled out and everything went black.

"**Quickly, secure** him!" Dr. Rhodes appeared through the door and darted to Commander Miller's unconscious form. "Thank you, Rachel, for your help on this one."

"Do you think he recognized me?" she asked. "Right before he was sedated, he called out my real name. He looked right at me and said Rachel instead of Krissy."

"Wouldn't that be something. We never inserted any of your father's recent memories of you in his consciousness. There's no way he'd recognize you as you are now, but we've never been this successful before. It's a pity his mind tried to revert back this morning. I wonder why his memories didn't revert back along with it. You'd think the shock of seeing himself would have overpowered the treatment."

"I think he really believed he was my father. He really thought he was Charley Oakley."

The doctor smiled. "Isn't it fantastic? Think of all the ways we could use this. If we can change a man like Commander Miller and put him in the mind of one of his victims—a great man like your father, just think of how we could change the world. We could end this war. Make everyone believe in our cause willingly. Miss Oakley, your help was indispensable."

"It was my pleasure. Anything to help bring the man who killed my father and so many others to justice."

"Oh, we'll do so much more than that. We'll make him seek justice for us."

THE ARK OF
THE UNKNOWN

A sulfuric breeze stung my nostrils as I watched Francis clamp a loop tight around the neck of the creature. It flicked its tongue back into its crystallized snout and showed its sparkling, jagged teeth. She hadn't decided what to name it yet. Francis was usually clever at nomenclature. I, on the other hand, would probably call it a crystal lizard or glass salamander.

"Marco, take hold of the loop and cage it. Make sure you lock it properly this time," Francis commanded, passing me the handle holding the snared creature. It thrashed and glistened in the sunlight as I struggled to lead it toward the cage. The crate sensed the creature, opened, and sucked it in, severing the loop I'd held it by. I made sure to press the locking mechanism and then thumbed "return." The cage slowly lifted from the ground and began to glide back toward the ship to be stored safely.

"What's next, boss?" I asked anxiously. Our mission was reaching its final day. I looked up at the clear blue sky and listened to the swaying of tallgrass. A black hole was nearing the planet. Earthquakes and volcanoes would soon begin to wreak havoc on the world. The planet would eventually turn to magma, until meeting the event horizon where it would be absorbed by the monstrous black hole.

Francis catalogued the creature in her compact digital registry and searched for more life. We had very little time to get to every species before TerraCore would order us to leave. This assignment was particularly hard for me. I had fallen in love with the world we'd been assigned to. It was beautiful and lively, yet I knew I would have to say goodbye forever. TerraCore sought out planets in need. Worlds on the cusp of destruction and in a state of utter helplessness. When I joined Francis's team, it seemed like a job I would find meaning in. Yet, after every assignment, I was left with a feeling of emptiness. TerraCore was owned by the Galactic Peace Government. In every step of the process, government officials made it clear that they were saviors of the living beings on each planet, and at great expense to themselves. We were only allowed a finite time to save life on each planet. And if the life forms weren't deemed intelligent by the government, we would only be allowed to collect a mating pair. The longer I worked for TerraCore, the more I understood that our mission was less about preserving life and more about finding out how it could be utilized to turn a profit.

"Two miles to the north. Let's take it on foot so we can log the flora," Francis said.

I took out my digital registry and scanned what plants I could. Genetic code uploaded automatically to the ship's main computer and clones of the plants could be grown later for habitat. It was easier to replicate plants than animals. Their happiness usually consisted of light, air, nutrients—all the sorts of stuff Francis dealt with once they were onboard. Of course, that varied too. Ciathian lilies, for example, ate small creatures, like grigles, which have an extremely poisonous mucus membrane. The lilies would then expel cyanide. Francis kept one onboard the ship. TerraCore thought the plant might be useful. Grigles were cloned to keep the lily happy, but each batch would only survive a week. I don't think they liked living on a spaceship just to be fed to a plant. Francis always rolled her eyes when I told her my theories, but I always said there was more to grigles than people thought. Francis held her hand up, signaling me to stop and get low. Lofty amber wisps of grass swirled around us in the wind, concealing our presence. The rustle of the grass was soothing, yet my thoughts lingered on the bogey up ahead. I heard a low hum and looked at Francis for instruction. She pointed to the sky where small leathery creatures floated above us. Small sacs on their backs lifted them into the air and tiny wings hummed, navigating their route.

"What are those?" I asked.

"The sacs are filled with anhydrous ammonia," Francis answered, reading the digital device in her hand.

"Well, we best leave them alone, then," I said nervously. "I don't want my skin and eyes melted."

"I'm going to send a cage for a few," Francis said.

"Francis, look," I said, pointing to the small, floating creatures. One by one, they dropped from above, releasing their deadly gas and dropping toward us. The vapor they were expelling would seek water to react with, even if it was the water in our bodies.

"Run!" Francis yelled. I darted after Francis in a panic, dodging the little ballooned creatures. We made it down a hill and took shelter behind a group of boulders. "Okay, we should be clear of the gas," she said, breathing hard.

"That was close," I wheezed.

"There's something else just beyond these boulders."

"Does it look big on the scanner?" I whispered.

"Yes. Best stay prepared." My eyes instinctively found the scar across Francis's face where a Pithus panther clawed her face years before. It had healed well. But there was a pale slash across her dark face, starting just above her brow and running across her eye. I never understood why Francis

177

didn't bother to get it removed. It polluted her otherwise flawless face.

"Be still," she whispered. We crouched lower. "They're all around us." Francis unholstered her weapon, rising slowly from the cover of foliage. Then her serious and morose face turned cheerful. A rare smile spread over her lips and she motioned me up. "It's alright. Come, take a look."

We found ourselves surrounded by the most adorable creatures I had ever come across. Their eyes were large blue orbs, which looked at us in wonder. Their fur was velvety and puffed out. The backs of their heads were elongated and boney. They looked a little like an iba, a large-hooved creature from the prairies of Hepsut. One of them approached Francis, nudging its head softly against her shoulder as if to greet her warmly.

"They don't fear us," Francis said. She reached out her hand and pet the animal on the neck. It purred as if thanking her.

I was soon surrounded by the soft, downy nudges of three of the friendly beasts. "They sure are affectionate," I said hesitantly. The pleasant purrs of the hooved creatures filed the air. For the first time in years, I felt genuinely happy and at ease, but my happiness was soon replaced by utter sadness. "How are we going to choose?" I looked at Francis, who seemed to be having a similar thought, for her smile had dissolved and her face had morphed once more into that hardened, unfeeling expression I knew so well.

She stopped petting the creature that was nudging her arm and examined the field of animals in a studious and facilitative manner. "We'll take this one," she said without emotion, gesturing toward the creature at her shoulder, "and the three surrounding you. They seem like the leaders."

"But that's more than a mating pair."

"Send for the cages," she instructed, moving out to log the surrounding plant life. I did as commanded and loaded the four creatures inside, one by one. A sudden rumble shook the ground. Earthquakes were becoming more prevalent each day. The cheerful purring stopped, replaced by confused screeching and moaning from the herd as their four comrades gently glided away toward the ship above. Fear of something new and unknown grew in the faces and noises of the animals.

"Our time is up," Francis said. Our pod appeared and I followed Francis in. The cries of the creatures grew louder and more desperate. One tried to enter the pod, whining and nudging me as if begging me to take it. Another creature tossed its foal inside the pod. The helpless creature yelped out for its mother as the pod lifted from the ground, leaving all others behind. The door sealed and I felt the familiar upward motion of the aircraft taking off. The foal cried softly in my arms as we left the world it knew. From the window, I could see the herd still and observant below, as if they knew we were their last hope. Usually animals run in fear, hide, or lash out at something foreign. They just stared, and I back at them, until they grew blurry and indiscernible, and the world they called home grew smaller and smaller in my view. Hopelessness overwhelmed me at the thought of their fate. The pod left the exosphere and the weightlessness of space gently lifted the foal and me from our seat. The creature let out a sharp cry at this new phenomenon. I looked to Francis, who remained unflapped.

"Do you think they knew what was going on?" I asked.

"Of course not," Francis answered. "We were told this planet had no intelligent life. And...we didn't see any." There was a hint of uncertainty in her voice, but she continued to guide the craft out.

I looked at the horrified creature in my arms and tears floated and swirled from my eyes.

Onboard the ship, I began moving the crated animals from the loading area to their respective places. Francis prepared their habitats, addressing which plants would need to be replicated where and what the exact climate should be for the health of each animal. But before the plants could be replicated and the animals introduced to their new homes, a manager from TerraCore had to give us the final approval. This was always the hardest part for me. Some unfeeling corporate goon might disapprove of the animals we had just spent weeks capturing, or he may deem them impractical and not worth the cost, and Francis would have to go back to the surface and release a portion of our work. I hated TerraCore managers, and I was pretty sure Francis did too. Whenever one came, her fists would ball up tightly until the manager left.

"Are they all in place?" she asked.

"This is the last load," I said, rolling a crate to the door of the enclosure.

A buzz sounded and Francis's hands coiled into fists. "Francis, how are we today?" Wiggins, the eldest and most condescending of the TerraCore managers stepped through the docking door. He never addressed me. To him I was nothing more than another one of Francis's pets or some lackey soon to be tossed out with all the other worn-out rubbish. It didn't matter that I had worked with Francis for five years and TerraCore six. I was a PS-235 dirtbag. Not like Francis; she had "good" blood. She grew up on Terra-1 and her parents were some sort of politicians.

"And how are your parents?" Wiggins asked, as if he knew it was a sore subject.

"Everything and everyone are fine, sir."

"Good to hear," he answered without seeming to mean it. "And what do we have here?"

"These are the last of the creatures we collected from the planet."

Wiggins took out his log and scrolled through it a minute. I could see Francis's eyes narrowing in on him. "Yes, you took five of these creatures here." He gestured toward the crates of the cheerful hooved animals. "Why?"

"It seemed like the right choice at the time. They are highly social animals and I believe they need more companionship. They...they seemed reactive to the earthquake...in a way that seemed to almost indicate intelligence or at least knowledge of what is coming to them."

"How would they know what's coming to them?"

"I don't know. It just seemed like they might understand that their world is dying. Like they understood they needed help to escape."

"Like they understood," Wiggins said with a smile. "Hey! You in there!" He pounded on the crates holding the creatures. "You going to write your memoirs on this experience?" The creatures shook, looking at Wiggins blankly. "Ah, just silly creatures. We found no evidence of any forms of intelligent life as described by the GPG guidelines for intelligence. Two is the norm for procreation, and of course they are only allowed to procreate if we think it appropriate."

"I have a doubt," Francis said. "I believe these creatures could be intelligent."

"Why do you always have to make things so difficult?" Wiggins scowled. "Did any creatures have a written language, grow crops, or share an organized religion?"

Francis said nothing but gave Wiggins a blistering stare.

"Two is still the rule," Wiggins said.

"I really believe at least these five—"

"No, lose three of them."

"Fine," she said abruptly. "I'll take them back down."

"No, you don't have time. Mass extinction events will be happening within the next hour. There's not enough time for anyone to get there and back safely."

"Then we'll have to keep all five."

"No," he said coldly. "Space three of them and keep two. I don't want duplicity and I don't want more expense than needed. It gets put on my record when things aren't as they should be. Put them out the airlock and be rid of the problem."

"Space them? Are you nuts?" I said, looking at Francis for support. Her tightened fists unfurled and dropped.

Wiggins lifted his command module to his mouth and said, "Send cages 25, 26, and 27 to airlock 7B." The enclosure opened and the cages glided inside, opening. Two of the creatures slowly lurched out into the empty airlock followed by the frightened foal. They greeted each other warily. Wiggins turned and approached the airlock panel. I turned to look at the three terrified creatures, the tiny foal seeking shelter between the older companions. Wiggins clicked open the safety cover of the outer door lock.

One of the creatures turned its head toward me and a strange feeling overcame me. I felt as though it wanted me to understand something. My heart ached for them and I took a step toward Wiggins. But I was too late. Wiggins pressed the button, opening the airlock.

"No!" I yelled. My words slowed into a long hum. I suddenly was immobile and the world around me stopped in place and then sharply sped backward. I shook my head, confused, and saw Wiggins approach the airlock panel again. My mind was still trying to grapple with the sudden rewind when I heard a pop and saw Wiggins drop to his knees; a groan escaping his wretched mouth as he fell back with a thud. I looked at Francis. Her hands firmly gripped her gun.

"What the hell happened?" she asked, still aiming her weapon in the direction that Wiggins had stood a second before. "Did you feel as though time slowed and moved backward?"

I looked at her, not knowing how to describe the experience. We approached Wiggins in silence. He rested in a heap on the floor, the corners of his mouth seeping red foam. Francis knelt beside him and felt his pulse. "Dead."

"But what happened?" I asked. "I saw him press the button and then it was as though we skipped back again."

Francis turned toward the creatures in the airlock.

"Them?" I asked. "You think they did it?" I turned to see one of the creatures in the airlock looking down at us through the glass, and a chill ran up my spine.

"Let them out of there," she commanded.

I gave her a look of uncertainty. I wanted no harm to come to the creatures but feared what they might be capable of.

"If it was them, they were just trying to defend themselves," Francis answered. "Besides, they didn't actually kill anyone. The killer is already on the same side of the glass as you."

I opened the door and the creatures approached, nuzzling us kindly. "TerraCore," I said. "How are we going to explain this?"

"They won't find out," Francis said. "I'm going to take Wiggins's ship to the surface."

"But it's too dangerous now," I said. "He said extinction events would occur within the next hour."

"I don't care anymore," Francis said with fire in her eyes. "We always do as we're told, and things suffer and die. I'm going down to the surface to get the rest of the herd we met. And I'm going to dump Wiggins's body."

"How would you explain that?" I asked. "He died trying to help you rescue a species? Anyone who knew him would know it was a lie."

"It's the only story I have."

"I'm coming with you," I said.

"No," Francis said. "If I don't make it back, you need to be here to take care of the animals."

"I can't take care of them myself," I said. "You could. Maybe I should go to the surface instead."

"We don't have time for a debate!" Francis yelled. She took hold of Wiggins's arms and dragged him through the docking door.

I headed to the helm to prepare to get away before the event horizon got too near and to pray that Francis would return. Getting to know Francis was a chore, but I had grown to love her. Not in a romantic sense, or at least not that I could comprehend at the time, but I loved her as a friend and companion. I couldn't imagine the ship or my life without her. It's true that she bossed me around and made me feel like absolute shit at times, but there were moments where another side of her came through. There was a compassionate side that was so courageous and loving, that you couldn't help but feel moved.

"Undocking and heading toward the planet," Francis said over the intercom.

"I'll be up here...praying," I replied. I felt a soft blow of warm air on my neck and turned to see the little foal standing behind me. "She's going to try her best," I spoke to it as though it understood my words.

I scanned space and began to monitor the movement of the black hole. The planet was on the verge of major gravitational disruption. My palms began to sweat, and I feared the worst. A call was incoming on the ship's communicator and I leaned over to see another TerraCore ship approaching.

"Hello, Wiggins. Come in." My throat tightened. "Where the hell are you going?"

I swallowed hard and replied, "Hello, this is Marco with the TerraCore Ark Project."

"What the hell is Wiggins doing heading toward the planet? I spoke with him only minutes ago and he was to join me in the Terra-5 zone. We all need to leave the area."

I knew I had to answer quickly, or he'd see through the charade. "He, uh, is going down to the surface to save an intelligent species."

"Save a species?" the voice sounded angry. "There's no intelligent life on this planet." The foal next to me snorted as if in disagreement.

"He agreed that there was and wanted to go back down and collect as many as possible," I answered.

"This sounds very unlike Wiggins. Why aren't they answering my calls?"

"Probably busy focusing on the task at hand," I said.

"I'm coming aboard. Prepare to be docked."

I fidgeted nervously. "Of course," I said, getting to my feet. The plan could still go smoothly even if another Terra-Core goon boarded the ship. I quickly called Francis. "Francis, we've got company up here," I said. "A TerraCore ship is preparing to dock."

"Show him a good time," she said, tersely. "I found the herd. I shouldn't be long."

"Stay here," I said to the little foal. I searched for the other hooved creatures and placed them all in an empty cargo room. "We'll get you more comfortable accommodations when Francis gets back. For now, stay here." I left the animals and headed down the main hall to the docking area. I could hear the docking mechanism outside the hall as I waited. The door opened shortly after and the TerraCore manager entered.

"What's all this nonsense about them needing to go to the surface, and why don't they answer my calls, yet respond to yours?"

"What do you mean they respond to mine?"

"I saw that Wiggins's ship took a call from you," he answered.

"Hmm…" I said, expelling air. I had forgotten they could see that. "I didn't call them. I've been too busy preparing the ship to leave. There's a black hole nearing this location, you know."

"What are you trying to hide?"

"I'm not hiding anything," I said, shrugging. The man brushed by me and went over to the airlock panel where Francis had shot Wiggins.

"What's this?" he asked. My heart pounded in my ears as I turned to see him inspecting the pool of blood leftover from Wiggins's corpse.

"Oh, one of the animals got injured," I said.

The man looked at me a moment and took his scanner out. "It says it's human."

"Really?" I said, shaking my head.

He stood inspecting the open door. "Did you know there's a database of blood profiles for every TerraCore employee?"

"Oh?" I said, tepidly. I then recalled the fingerpick and the upload of my blood sample to a program.

"So, if I start thinking something seems a bit suspicious. I could have this analyzed."

"Oh, come on. Calm down," I said. "I cut myself on accident all the time. It's probably mine."

"I can see through you, Marco," he said. He walked around, inspecting the ship. "I know you do whatever Francis says. You've got no backbone." He was now inside the room with the airlock. I could get rid of him if I just walked toward the panel, closed him in, and opened the airlock. It would only take a moment.

"Is Wiggins really down there with Francis?" the man asked. I inched toward the panel, eyeing it as I neared. "Where is he?" the man's voice grew angry.

I tapped the button and the door closed, trapping the man inside. His eyes widened. "What are you doing, Marco!" he yelled, banging on the glass. "Let me out of here!" A lump grew in my throat. I didn't want to do it. I didn't want to hurt him, but he was giving me no choice. "Don't!" he yelled. My hand froze over the controls to the airlock door.

"You don't have to!" Francis shouted, suddenly running into the room.

"You're back," I said, letting my hand fall to my side.

"Leave him in there for now, until we can figure out what to do with him."

I nodded. "Did you get the herd?" I asked.

"Yes, and a few more," Francis said.

"What do you mean more?" I asked. Francis showed me through to where she had docked Wiggins's ship. It was packed with the furry, hooved creatures. A few standing on chairs and some on the tops of enclosures filled with other species of animals. Strange growls and purrs clamored throughout the ship and it smelled of grass and dirt.

"I went a little crazy and just saved everything I saw," she said, shrugging.

"Where are we going to house all of them?" I asked.

"We'll figure it out," Francis said. "For now, we need to get them all on our ship before we get pulled apart by this black hole."

"They could probably just rewind time before that happened."

"I wouldn't count on that against a black hole," Francis said. "They came very willingly. I think they know they can't help their planet."

I smiled.

"What?" she said.

"Now you've got theories that there's more to an animal than we think," I said.

"Come on," Francis said. "Let's get going."

"Where to after we get them all inside?" I asked.

"I don't know," she said. "We should probably find a suitable place for them to live. They won't be able to stay on the ship forever. And we need to find a place to dump the TerraCore guy in the airlock."

"You mean space him?" I asked, worried.

"No," Francis said. "I've already killed one person today, let's try not to go homicidal. We'll figure out some way of keeping him quiet."

"I'm so glad you made it back," I said, giving her a hug.

"Alright, alright, let's get to it," Francis said, pushing me off and motioning the creatures to board the ship. I watched the little foal run and greet its mother with a happy shriek.

We had killed one TerraCore manager and kidnapped another. Francis and I were never going to get away with it. Our relationship with TerraCore was over. We had become galactic outlaws. But as I watched the hooved animals purring in thanks as they entered our ship, I didn't care. I was proud to be an outlaw.

VIOLENT MESSENGERS

I was never prepared for the otherworldliness of the Antarctic winter. Its dark, magical sky and endless stretches of snow—where sastrugi formed in minutes to create obstacles underfoot, where frostbite could set in with frightening speed, and katabatic winds blasted minus seventy-degree Celsius temperatures. It was no place for the fragile, yet humans chose this location for some of the most sensitive observatories.

I fidgeted nervously as I waited in the galley at the Amundsen-Scott South Pole Station. I was there to write about the science and day-to-day life during the winter season. I had been a journalist for over fifteen years, racking up bylines in every environmental and science publication out there. Antarctica had always been interesting to me, and I recognized the importance of sharing the work being done there with the public. The assignment also offered me distance and time away from a world I had begun to resent.

"Hello, Ms. Dolivo," a woman said. I looked up to see Dr. Lucy Freling staring down at me. She was in her late fifties with dark speckled gray hair and a judicious expression. This was Dr. Freling's second year as an overwinterer at the station. Her list of accomplishments was long. She worked with the team that discovered the absolute mass of the neutrino. Known as "ghost particles," the neutral subatomic particles are hard to detect and rarely interact with matter. The absolute mass of the neutrino remained a mystery years after it was discovered. But the neutrino could change its type, or as those in the physics community call it, its flavor—something a particle can only do if it has mass. I didn't know what brought Dr. Freling to Antarctica at the time. I thought perhaps there was a breakthrough at the IceCube Neutrino Observatory or maybe it was the vast stars or the green aurora that moved like magical green ribbons in the sky that drew her to the snowy continent. Antarctica was a place of mystery that made you feel close to science. If you were studying the cosmos, you could look up and see more stars than you ever imagined. It made the mysteries of space seem more obtainable, yet more infinite.

"It is Annie Dolivo, right?" Dr. Freling asked, noticing my aloofness.

"Oh, yes. I'm sorry," I answered. "I've been a bit absent-minded today."

"Winter here can do that to you. Not having any sunlight can make your brain fuzzy. Have you tried the gym? I saw they have a yoga class tomorrow." She looked up at the screen across the galley. "Looks like Andy is teaching it. I might go to that. Sounds fun."

"I should try it," I said, giving her a grin.

"Oh, here comes Emily," she said, waving at a younger woman who was walking back from the cookie bar. "Get yourself a snack?"

"It's too hard. They always have these cookies out and I can't resist," she said, just before biting into the large choc-olate chip confection in her hand. Emily was young and wide-eyed with a sweet smile and an inquisitive brow.

"Emily, this is Annie Dolivo," Dr. Freling said. "She's going to be joining us at the ICL."

"I've watched your show on the news. I enjoy it," Emily said, putting her cookie down on the table to give me an en-thusiastic handshake.

"I'm glad someone watches it," I said. I always tried to let compliments slide off me like an unwanted garment.

"Oh, I think a good portion of America watches it," Emily said. "I really enjoyed your piece on SETI and METI. You were pretty tough on that METI guy."

I swallowed and tried not to let my uneasiness show. My interview with the SETI Institute, a group known for their search for extraterrestrial intelligence, had gone smoothly for the most part, but when I began interviewing a young man with METI, a group who sends messages out into space in the hope that someone will answer, I had gone off the rails. I was known for being tough. I once made a dangerous politician from the East sweat through his shirt with my persistent questions. But the METI interview was with an eager young student, and he cried, and my producers ran with it.

"I agree with what you said. Maybe we should not be beaconing ourselves. You never know who will answer the call...the one who answers could be dangerous." Emily picked her cookie up again and took a bite. "But did you really have to call him an optimistic little fool?"

"No, I shouldn't have, and I regret saying it," I said. I gave a shrug and looked toward Dr. Freling for instruction.

"Emily is a postdoc from Illinois," Dr. Freling said with a laugh. She ran a hand through her hair. "Well, I think it's time to suit up. It's minus seventy-five Celsius and the windchill will make it feel like minus ninety."

"How long does the walk generally take?" I asked, getting to my feet and following the two women from the galley.

"Well, that all depends," Dr. Freling sighed. "It's about one kilometer or two-thirds of a mile from the station. It could take ten minutes, or it could take closer to twenty-five minutes. I'm thinking with the low visibility we have today, it'll be closer to twenty-five." My shoes squeaked on the station floors as we walked through the hallways until reaching the coat room where our ECW, extreme cold weather gear, was kept. I secured my layers and ensured I had no exposed skin, then attached my face mask and goggles.

The three of us exited through the Hercules door—a thick metal door with a long handle that latched like a freezer door. We were indeed entering the world's largest freezer. I couldn't help but think of Narnia and little Lucy Pevensie venturing through the wardrobe into an eternal winter. The wind howled through the dark expanse before me, pelting snow at my body. I heard a faint call from Dr. Freling as my ears adapted to the noise, but her words were lost in the wind. I walked nearer to make out what she was saying and suddenly found myself face-down in the hard snow. My muscles tightened as a shiver ran down my spine. With a large exhalation and a shake of my head, I forced myself to my feet once more.

"I was trying to tell you to only walk on the left side of these flags today," she said, helping me from the ground. "The snow on the left has been groomed and is easier to walk on."

"Got it," I said, keeping close to Dr. Freling. Emily followed behind. Visibility was greatly reduced due to the extreme wind sweeping up snow and I found myself wondering if it was safe to be out and if the weather was going to get worse. I tried to see the arm of the Milky Way or a banner of green aurora, but only saw a white haze of snow. Walking was slow and cumbersome, and I could not make out any structures ahead.

"A little farther and we'll be walking over the neutrino detector!" Dr. Freling yelled over the wind. "It's a one square kilometer detector…or telescope under the surface of the lab. It has digital detectors called DOMs attached by strings through boreholes. It's designed to detect high energy neutrinos."

"Astrophysical neutrinos," Emily shouted from behind. "Like those produced from supernova, gamma rays, and black holes."

"How far down do the boreholes go? Will we hurt anything by walking on it?" I asked.

"Their depths vary but they go down as far as 2,500 meters. We can't hurt anything by walking on it. The ice is so thick."

I looked at the snow under my feet and tried hard to picture such a structure reaching a mile and a half under the frozen world. A spot on my wrist began to burn. I held up my hand and tightened my mitten. My skin immediately felt relief. A faint yelp from ahead of us echoed through the wind. As we continued, I spotted a small seal wiggling on the snow. The other two women pointed and shook their heads as they walked by. I paused, looking over at the poor doomed creature with pity. It wrenched my stomach to know the innocent and cute animal was about to die and that we were forbidden to help it. "Come on, Annie!" I heard Dr. Freling yell. "We can't do anything for it." Seals occasionally went astray, making the slow and cumbersome trek inland near the station instead of toward the sea. What a lonely journey it would be through the cold and gloom. They would cry out when they sensed human movement, unsure of us but acknowledging that they were no longer alone. I was certain they were asking for help, food, water, or even directions. But we were supposed to let nature take its course. Over time, the seal would become nothing more than a mummified pelt in the snow. I trudged by the poor creature, leaving it to its fate.

After a little while, I began to see a faint trace of light ahead. It took several more minutes for the exterior of the IceCube Neutrino Observatory to fade into visibility. It was a two-story square building with two arms stretched out from each side connecting to two pillars. Stairways crisscrossed the exterior of the building.

Emily let me by, and I followed Dr. Freling up the stairs. Inside, we immediately began pulling our gear off and hung it to dry and warm near the door.

"There's a small counter over there with a few snacks and beverages if you need anything," Dr. Freling said, pointing. "Off to the side over there is where we house cargo, and around the corner is the electronics lab where Emily will be making some repairs. I usually join her, but since you are here, we thought that I could show you around a bit first." We left Emily to her work and I followed Dr. Freling through an inner stairwell to the second floor of the lab.

"This is the control room," she said, showing me through to a small room with a pair of long desks and a few computer screens. "This is where we do the computer tasks and check on the DOMs."

"What exactly are the DOMs?"

"The DOMs, or Digital Optical Modules, are photodetectors, about the size of a basketball, that allow us to detect the neutrinos from underneath the ice. They're what's attached to the cords under the ice that send us info." Dr. Freling pointed toward a poster on the wall showing a spherical device. The device did remind me of a basketball, one which was divided into a top and bottom. The bottom of the device looked like it had lightbulbs under a transparent gold covering and the top was clear showing innards of electronic circuits and wires.

"How do they detect neutrinos?"

Dr. Freling leaned over and turned on the computer to her right. "When an astrophysical neutrino strikes a particle of normal matter—which doesn't happen very often since they aren't very reactive and can move through the cosmos in a straight line for light-years without ever interacting with anything—but on the occasion that a neutrino does interact, it produces secondary particles that emit light called Cherenkov light, and the DOMs collect the light. This info is sent to the computers up here on the surface."

Dr. Freling spoke with exactness, yet she was very enthusiastic. This woman was genuinely excited to share her work. It was comforting to know that there were still people in love with their work. "The computers translate the messages from each DOM into light patterns and show the direction and energy of the neutrino," Dr. Freling continued. "This means we can tell where it originated. One hundred trillion neutrinos pass through you every second. So, they're very abundant. There's only a small chance that a neutrino will react instead of pass through the Earth undetected. This is why it's very important to keep the lab up and running at all times. So that we are here when one does make contact with the ice. Would you like to see the server room?"

"I'd love to."

Dr. Freling paused and took a white jacket from a rack near the door. "This looks about your size," she said, handing me the jacket. "When we enter the server room, we have to put them on. They reduce static electricity. Despite the snow everywhere, we're in the driest desert on the planet, so there can be a lot of static buildup and it messes with the equipment." A tangy, synthetic smell made my throat tighten as I pulled the jacket on. But I kept the coat on and followed Dr. Freling inside the server room. The whirl of machinery buzzed in my ears as we entered.

"It's cooler in here than the rest of the lab," I said over the hum of the servers.

"One of the hardest parts of my job is keeping the server room at the appropriate temperature. Too hot and things overheat, too cold and things start to crack."

"They can get too hot here?"

Dr. Freling laughed. "I know. Crazy."

"What are all these wires?"

"The thick gray cables are tapped into the ice and connected to the DOMs. They connect to these red wires."

"So many red wires." I looked about the room. There were bundles upon bundles of red wires leading into servers.

"The red wires connect to the DOM hubs. See those servers behind the red wires?" I nodded. "Each DOM hub is connected to one string of DOMs. One string is 60 DOMs in the ice."

"It's so strange to think of all these computers out here in the middle of Antarctica," I said. "Is there much happening during the winter, or are you and Emily just making sure it stays in working order?" Dr. Freling's expression changed into what I could only describe as hollow.

"The neutrinos we are looking for get detected about once a month, but nothing substantial yet," she replied. "The summer months are good for updates and changes to the lab. We are basically just keeping it in working order right now. Come on, let's leave this noise behind." Dr. Freling showed me through the door and sat in front of a computer. I pulled up a chair and took a seat next to her. There was silence as she booted up the system.

"This is your second winter in Antarctica, isn't it?" I asked, filling the silence.

"Yes," she said with a sigh. "I don't mind the winters. It is quiet. The stars are beautiful. And you get plenty of time to think and find new hobbies."

"Do you think about research for the summer?"

"I think about any number of things," she answered, typing into the keyboard.

"I'm curious why someone as renowned as you would be overwintering here and for a second year." I shifted in my seat, trying to pick my words wisely. "It seems like most are younger and not as accomplished in their field yet. What keeps bringing you back to babysit the observatory in winter?"

"This job is very sought-after and very challenging, mentally and physically. It's nothing to downgrade. A lot of people want this position."

"Of course," I replied. "I didn't mean to offend. Many of the tasks are far beyond my comprehension. I know little about physics and don't know much about the computer-based tasks needed to keep IceCube running. It is an important job and there's no doubt about that. I only meant that it would seem like a wonderful opportunity for someone like Emily. I mean, you were part of the team that won a Nobel Prize in your field. A team that discovered the absolute mass of the neutrino. Don't you have important research to get to?"

"I enjoy working here," she answered. She turned from her computer screen to look at me.

"I heard there were fewer people allowed to conduct research and updates here this summer. They were planning on an upgrade with a different kind of DOM and it didn't happen."

"The mDOMs weren't put in this year as planned. Hopefully next summer."

I sighed and sat back in my chair. "If something new gets detected, what's the procedure?"

"This screen is a live monitor of the DOMS," she said. "It tells us if something has happened and it transfers data to the north."

"So data from the observatory is shared in real time?"

"It is very near real time. The trigger will go through filters first and then data is sent by either satellite, secure copy, or email."

The door to the control room creaked open and Emily appeared. "How's it going in here?" she asked as she sat down at one of the computers.

"Good," answered Dr. Freling. "Just checking in with the system."

"I finished with the hard drives."

"Good," said Dr. Freling.

"Have you already shown Miss Dolivo the server room?"

"Yes."

"Pretty neat, huh?" she said, looking at me.

"Very," I said. "And you can call me Annie."

The phone rang and Emily got up and answered. "Hello," she said. "Oh. Got it. Are you bringing a vehicle?" Emily shifted on her feet as she listened. "Well, we appreciate it. Thank you." Emily hung up the phone and turned to Dr. Freling and me. "Looks like the weather is going to get pretty bad and they want people to get back to the station now. Bryce is coming to pick up Annie. Unfortunately, something is wrong with the PistenBully so he's only got a snowmobile."

"Does that mean he has to come back for you two after I go?" I said, looking at Emily.

"He can only safely fit one person on the snowmobile. There is a trailer he could tow on the back, but I don't feel comfortable going in it with this wind. We could always stay here and ride it out if it gets too bad, but I thought you might want to get back."

"I would like to get back, if it's safe enough for Bryce to drive out here and back."

"Oh, I'm sure it'll be fine," said Dr. Freling. "You better start getting your gear on. He'll be here soon." I went down to the first floor and began putting my extreme weather gear on. As soon as I placed my goggles over my eyes there was a knock on the door.

"That must be your ride," Dr. Freling said, appearing from around the corner.

"Thank you for showing me around," I said, getting to my feet. "I hope the weather calms down soon."

"Be careful," Dr. Freling said, patting me on the shoulder. "We'll see you back at the station." Bryce met me outside the door and showed me to the idling snowmobile.

"Thanks for coming, Bryce," I yelled over the wind.

"No problem," he said as I sat down behind him on the vehicle. "Hold on tight. It's windy as hell." I clutched my mittens around the handles on the back of the snowmobile and held my breath as we started to move swiftly through the blankets of blowing snow. Conditions had worsened since our walk to the ICL. I could see nothing in front of us as we raced over the white icy terrain.

"How do you know you're going the right way?" I asked.

"I've got my GPS and…" Bryce was cut off, and I was suddenly thrown from the vehicle. I flew through the air and landed hard in the snow. My right shoulder throbbed, and my thoughts raced. Rolling around on the frozen ground, I tried wrapping my mind around what happened. I got to my feet, fearful of my circumstances. I looked around for Bryce, but the wind was kicking up too much snow and I could see nothing. "Bryce!" I yelled in a panic. I hobbled over to where I thought the vehicle may be but saw only snow. "Bryce!" I yelled out once more. This time I heard a faint groan from somewhere behind me. I turned. "Bryce, keep saying something!" Another groan, this time louder, sounded just ahead of me. I followed the noise and found Bryce sprawled out on the ground.

"Are you okay?" I asked, kneeling beside him.

"My leg hurts," he gasped. "It's hard to put any weight on it."

"We need to find the vehicle." I placed Bryce's arm over my shoulder, and we struggled about in search of the vehicle.

"I think we hit a big snowdrift," Bryce said. "I saw it and overcorrected to miss it."

"The road has gotten pretty treacherous."

"There…there's the snowmobile," he said, pointing. I helped Bryce to the ground and struggled to get the vehicle off its side. It took me several attempts, but I was finally able to get it upright.

"It turned off," I said.

"Damn," Bryce answered. "Try starting it back up."

I tried the ignition several times to no avail. "It's dead."

"The engine got too cold. Let's try and radio someone at the station," Bryce said. Bryce patted his coat. "My radio is gone. It must have fallen off somewhere when I fell. Can you radio in?"

"I…" that horrible feeling that comes along whenever I've been stupid and careless welled up in the pit of my stomach. "I must have forgotten mine at the ICL."

"You forgot yours?" Bryce's voice sounded angry.

"I'm sorry," I said, knowing it was a stupid mistake.

"Well, let's look around and see if we can find mine. Maybe it's not far." I helped Bryce to his feet, and we retraced our steps in search of the radio. "No good. We'll just have to head back to the ICL. We can call someone there. At least we aren't far from the lab," he wheezed.

"Is the pain in your leg really bad?"

"I think I may have broken something."

"We'll get back and see if someone can come get you."

Bryce put his weight on my shoulder. I struggled to find firm footing on the snowy ground as the wind beat us back. We found the flags and followed them closely so as not to lose our way. "I can see the lab," I said. The ICL could be

R.A. Hogan

seen faintly through blasts of snow breeze. We approached
the lab and I struggled to find the way to the stairs. We were
lost in a white world of snow and freezing wind. By luck, we
finally found the stairwell and I helped Bryce up the stairs
until we reached the door and found our way inside. I shed
my gloves and goggles and took a deep breath of the sterile
and warm air inside the lab. I led Bryce to a chair in the little
kitchen area and helped him take his cold weather gear off
to inspect his leg. As I stripped his sock from his foot, I immediately noticed tissue swelling around the ankle bone. "It
looks pretty bad. It is starting to bruise." I thought back to
my required medical training before coming to the station. I
tried rotating the ankle and found movement limited.

"I can put weight on it," Bryce gasped. "It just hurts."

"Did you hear a pop or crack?" I asked.

"I only heard the wind," Bryce answered.

"Well, since it's already bruising, and you could put
weight on it, I think it might be a sprain, but try not to put
weight on it until we can get to the clinic."

"Can I have something to drink?" he asked. I poured him
a cup of warm tea and handed it to him. "Thanks."

"I'm going to go find the others and let them know what
happened," I said. Bryce nodded and sipped his drink.

I walked up the interior stairwell until I reached the door
to the control room. I knocked and quickly opened the door.
Dr. Freling was sitting at a computer and Emily stood behind
her, blocking my view of the screen. "You're back?" Emily
said, bewildered. "What happened?"

"We had an accident. Bryce injured his leg."

"Bad?"

"It's pretty swollen."

208

"The snowmobile?"

"Wouldn't start. We had to walk back here. It was closer than the station."

"Does he think his leg is broken?" Dr. Freling asked, peeking from behind Emily.

"Not sure. I think it might be a sprain."

"Let me call and see if anyone can come get him to the infirmary. Maybe another vehicle is ready now," Emily said, picking up the ICL phone.

"Were you able to radio anyone?" Dr. Freling asked. "We never heard the radio here."

I shook my head. "No, Bryce lost his and, uh, I forgot mine here," I said, looking down.

"Well, I'm glad you both made it back," Dr. Freling answered. She got to her feet. "We better go have a look at him." I followed her to where I left Bryce. "How's the leg, Bryce? I heard you had an accident."

"Yeah," Bryce grunted. "Hit a damn snowdrift. I'm pretty sure I got lucky and it's just a sprain." As Dr. Freling bent down to have a look, Emily came flying through the door.

"Well," Emily said, "looks like we're staying here tonight. They still can't get the PistenBully going and the wind is supposed to get worse. Might as well make ourselves comfortable. Bryce, you can have the cot in the bunk room since you're hurt."

"Thanks," Bryce sighed. "I wouldn't mind just hanging around with you all for a while. My adrenaline is pumping pretty fast and I need a moment to calm down."

"I hope we can find the snowmobile when the storm stops," Emily said.

"Me too," Bryce said.

"I'm sure we'll be able to find it," Dr. Freling said, reassuringly.

"Here." Emily handed Bryce a cookie and sat next to him. "Want to play cards or something?"

"Sure," Bryce said, with a slight smile. "I'd like that. If you aren't busy."

"We've done all our tasks for the day," Emily answered. I watched Dr. Freling move toward one of the windows. She took the piece of cardboard covering the window off and looked outside. I approached and stopped next to her to inspect the storm. "Have you ever seen a storm this bad?"

"I haven't seen one come so quickly," she sighed. "It wasn't supposed to get like this until tomorrow."

"We'll be okay here, right?"

"Yeah, we'll be okay. They'll get the PistenBully started again soon and we'll be back at the station in the morning." Dr. Freling continued looking out into the white swirling snow. "We won't be seeing any stars or aurora tonight."

"Is that what keeps bringing you back here, the night sky?"

"I think several things attract me to this place."

"You don't have family at home who miss you?"

"I did," she said, turning from the window and seating herself at a nearby chair.

"Did something happen?"

"Are you interviewing me or asking as a friend?"

I looked over the impressive woman seated before me. "I would like to be your friend. But I think people would like to read about you too."

"I don't usually enjoy talking about my personal life," she said.

"If you want to talk to me as a friend and don't want me to write about something, I won't."

"I have read a few of your books," Dr. Freling said, studying me. "And watched your show. I know you don't get ahead by holding back."

"That's not the real me," I said. I noticed my hands were still shaking—leftover nerves from the accident.

"What's the real you, then?"

I turned to the window and looked out onto the snow. "I don't enjoy my work anymore and it's all I've become. I'm like a star in the night sky, I shine beside too many others, and no one cares who I am. I'm not unique. No one is unique. We all just say and do what others have already done. I don't even have control of what I get to publish or say anymore, and it doesn't matter because someone has already thought or said everything.

"When I look up in the night sky, I wish I could just float off to one of those specks up there. Maybe there's a place that understands the mistakes we're making or an alternate reality where I kept trying. I just want to find a place where I can feel like me again." It felt good to talk to someone. For so long, I had kept my feelings under wraps. It took the most desolate place on the planet to break down my walls. I tried to imagine the picturesque sky above the white clouds of snow as I looked out.

"You know," Dr. Freling said, getting to her feet to stand next to me at the window, "on a clear night here you can go out and get lost just looking up. It doesn't matter if you know every constellation, what's a planet and what's not. The stars are so incredibly plentiful here that there's no way to know every single little speck. But every astronomer knows they are unique.

"I suppose some people would feel small and insignificant when they looked at all the stars. But it should make us feel unique. Out of all those specks, we haven't found one with life yet. And if we ever do find life somewhere else, maybe it'll make us realize how rare it is.

"And to answer your question," Dr. Freling sighed and looked toward me. "I have no one who misses me back home. My husband died a few years ago. It is a big part of why I've overwintered here twice."

"I'm sorry," I said, meeting her gaze.

"It's okay," Dr. Freling said, turning her attention back to the storm outside. "I can't say I personally believe in an afterlife. But it is hard to believe someone you loved so deeply would cease to be anything. Just lived and was, and then poof—nothing. No, when I look up into the stars, I can feel him. He may not be in the heaven they taught me about in Sunday school, but he's part of everything still. Just like you and me. We are made of the stuff out there in the cosmos and someday small particles of us will return to the cosmos. Working here reminds me of that." A few moments passed as we both watched the blizzard from the window before Dr. Freling added, "And I'd like to be your friend."

"I'd like that too," I said, smiling.

A beep sounded, and I jerked my head away from the window. I looked at Dr. Freling. "Event alert," she said, her eyes widening.

Dr. Freling went toward the stairwell and Emily followed. "I want to have a look too," Bryce said, setting a hand of cards down on the table where he and Emily had been playing. I went to Bryce and helped him up, his arm flung around my shoulder, and we made our way up the stairs. By the time we made it to the control room, Dr. Freling and Emily were already studying their monitors. I let Bryce rest in a chair and caught my breath.

"What is it?" Bryce asked.

"We got a trigger," Emily said, peering at the computer screen in front of her. Another alert sounded. "Oh, another one." Emily's brow furrowed.

"I thought you only detected a neutrino about once a month," I said, confused.

"Let's see what the processing farm says. Okay…" Dr. Freling leaned back in her chair, combing a hand through her hair as she studied the screen before her. "Emily, you see this?"

"This is insane," Emily said. There was a long pause. I sat dumbfounded, listening to a succession of alerts sound over the system. "We've detected 30 neutrinos. They're about 10 PeV!"

"PeV, what does that mean?" I asked.

"Their energy," Dr. Freling answered, sounding shocked. "It means they're cosmogenic neutrinos or ultra-high energy neutrinos." Dr. Freling turned to Emily. "I can't believe this."

"So where do those come from?" I asked.

Emily looked at me and then back at Dr. Freling, who answered, "We don't really know. That's why it's so extraordinary. The ICL has never detected neutrinos like this. We could learn things about the universe we couldn't even imagine from this detection."

"Like what?" I asked.

"A PeV is a quadrillion times more energetic than an electron volt…the energy it takes to move one electron. We aren't sure what might cause energies from a neutrino this high, but maybe a blazar, a quasar, hypersupernovae, gamma ray burst, a certain type of black hole."

"Heavy dark matter," Emily added.

"Maybe," Dr. Freling said. "It'll be exciting to see what telescopes can see and give us an idea of what it might be."

"What a night to be stuck in the ICL," Bryce said. "What about the storm? Has it messed with your uptime?"

"Still up," Emily said. "All our friends in the north have already been notified, and we should be able to know more about where it came from once telescopes and other observatories start looking in the direction the neutrinos came.

"It's extraordinary how they came in just one after another like that," Emily said. "Bryce, come look at the Cherenkov light patterns."

Bryce hobbled toward Emily, leaning over to look at her screen. "Would you look at that," he said, shaking his head. "So, looks like they all came from the same direction."

"I think so," Emily said.

I glanced over, seeing a rainbow of globular color among vertical strings representing the detector. "So that's the light produced when a neutrino hits the ice?" I asked.

"Yes," Emily said, smiling up at me. "It's a very faint blue light. You wouldn't be able to see it and the only way we can detect it is with the DOMs, and only because they're in such a dark, clear place—" Emily paused as the system sounded another alert. "It's detecting more," she said, confused.

214

"Hmm…interesting," Dr. Freling said. "Looks like they might be coming from the same direction too."

"Maybe a gamma ray burst of some kind," Emily said.

"They're coming in at the exact same time intervals between each neutrino arrival here as with the group that came in earlier."

"What does that mean?" I asked.

"I don't know," Dr. Freling said.

"What if it's binary," Bryce jested.

The women didn't laugh but continued looking over their monitors in silence. "Binary code," I said, flatly.

"I was only joking," Bryce said. "Don't destroy me like you did that METI kid."

I looked aghast at the other two. "Has everyone in Antarctica seen that interview?"

Bryce looked over at Emily. "Well, I might have shared it with a few people," Emily said. "I wasn't trying to make fun of you or anything." Emily's voice rose an octave. "It was more like, look, this lady might interview you…be prepared." She put her hands up disarmingly and then turned back to her computer.

"I've become a dragon lady," I said.

"Dragon ladies are fun, and unique," Dr. Freling said. "Come over here, I want you all to look at this." We all huddled around Dr. Freling's computer. "The first event happened at 7:08 and we detected 30 neutrinos. The last neutrino from the first event hit at 7:13. Then we had exactly 10 minutes between that and the time the second event began. The last neutrino from the second event was detected at 7:29. I'm curious to see if we may have another trigger at 7:39."

"Why would you think there would be another one?" asked Emily.

"Oh, I don't know," Dr. Freling said. "I doubt there will be…"

"You do think there could be a pattern?" Bryce asked.

"I didn't say that," Dr. Freling said, looking around at everyone in the room. "I think we should pay attention to what we already have and see what everyone in the north says. It could be some sort of flaring event or burst occurring out in space. I'm only curious to see if another trigger occurs at 7:39. I probably shouldn't have even said anything."

"It's 7:36 now," Emily said. The group sat in silence, watching, waiting. I couldn't help but feel the notion of waiting on a signal to arrive from the outer reaches of space at a very specific time was a bit far-fetched, if not even crazy, but I respected Dr. Freling.

"7:39," Emily said, looking at her monitor. "Nothing." Her shoulders sunk. "Well, we still detected something—" There was a beep and Emily sat up.

"And we've got another trigger," Dr. Freling said, shaking her head.

I stood, amazed. I looked over to see Bryce jumping up and down, momentarily forgetting his injury. He fell, laughing softly and holding his leg.

"It'll certainly be interesting to find out where these are coming from. Let's see how many this time…" After a few minutes, it was clear that another 30 neutrinos had been detected. We waited for another trigger, for another 30 neutrinos, but they never came.

"Have any other observatories gotten back to you?" I asked.

"Not yet," Dr. Freling answered. "I guess we'll have to wait and see."

"I wonder if Super K in Japan detect them," Emily said.

"I hope so," Dr. Freling said.

The storm raged on and the detector remained silent. After a few hours of residual excitement, our anticipation began to wane. I watched Bryce and Emily play cards across the room and Dr. Freling work quietly at her computer. I took a white jacket from the entrance to the server room and curled up in a chair and gradually began to nod off. I slept. Uneasy, cold thoughts tossed through my mind, until floating away from the lab to a dreamland where violent explosions and burning suns gave birth to invisible particles.

"Annie," Dr. Freling's voice echoed softly above me. "The storm is gone."

"How long was I out?" I asked, rising from my chair, my neck stiff and achy. Dr. Freling was wearing her gear as if ready to leave.

"A few hours."

"Any news on the neutrinos you detected?"

Dr. Freling smiled. "Meet us on the snowdrift outside."

"What?" I asked.

"Get your gear on and meet us outside," she said, walking away. I went to the first floor and dressed in my ECW and went to meet them. It was early morning yet still dark, as it would be for several more months. The storm had passed and there was a peaceful silence drifting along the frigid air. I looked up to a clear night sky and saw stars. Unmeasurable specks highlighting the Milky Way and beyond. I spotted the other three seated on a snow drift just below. I climbed down the stairs and met them.

"Why are we all out here?" I asked.

"The storm stopped and it's a perfect time to take a look at the stars," Dr. Freling said.

"Why don't we head back to the station?" I asked. "Is there a vehicle coming?"

"The PistenBully is heading this way soon," Dr. Freling said.

"Bryce, how's the leg?" I asked.

"Not bad," he said. "I think some of the swelling has gone down."

"Any news about the neutrino event?" I asked. They all looked around at each other and I was certain they were smiling under their masks. "What?"

"It was a message," Dr. Freling said, leaning back in the snow to look up at the sky.

"It was binary code," Bryce said, laughing.

"A message," Emily added. "The Super K detected everything too."

Dr. Freling laughed loudly from her place on the snowdrift.

"How is that possible?" I asked, taking a seat on the cold snow. "A message through particles? Are you trying to pull one over on me? Is this a joke?"

"No, no," Dr. Freling said. I had never heard her voice so full of energy. "It's the truth."

"Then, it must have come from someone here on Earth," I said.

"Not possible," Dr. Freling answered. "We know the direction it came from and its energy isn't right for anything local. Neutrinos are born from some of the most violent events in the universe and these are such high energies."

"Well, then where?" I asked. "What did the telescopes see when they looked that way? Some sort of explosion?"

"Nothing," Dr. Freling said.

"What does that mean?" I asked. "I thought you said it would have to be a huge violent event to get neutrinos with those energies?"

"It means that our young civilization still has a lot to learn," Dr. Freling said.

"What kind of a message was this? Did it say something or—"

"It says, 'You are not alone,'" Emily said, pounding her feet into the snow.

I fell back, resting my head on the snow and looked up, searching the stars. "You are not alone," I repeated.

Afterword

In my short story "They," the plan was to engineer a world with characters that had lost the ability to question the world. I wanted to create a world where artificial intelligence had become so interlinked in the psyche of people that they were forgetting to live as we do now. I don't think it's very far-flung from the reality in which many are living today—where every post, happy or sad, superficial or deep, can be monetized and sponsored. Where a writer is only good if they have twenty-thousand followers on social media. Alice's tragedy was that she was unable to think for herself, even after her brief escape from the Connection. She believed in the system she knew to a fault, and this inability to separate herself from it inevitably led to her death. The story placed in the science fiction short story category at my state writing conference and has usually been pretty well received with the exception of a few people who didn't like Alice's lack of agency to overcome the system. I continue this theme of an artificial system taking over in "Tech Torrent," which is a prelude to my novel, *The Altridge Syndrome* (not yet published). In the novel, people are "infected" through their individual devices and become members of the Tech Torrents—a weaponized group controlled by A.I.

"Colfax County Coal" was a bit different from the other stories because it was inspired by a real place. The idea for the story came to me after I visited the ghost town of Dawson, NM—little more than a cemetery remains of the town today. Two horrible mining disasters occurred in the town and it was eventually demolished. Although I left it a bit ambiguous, the story is set in the late 1800s. Ambiguity can often be a mistake in short stories; however, I thought the era was laid out well enough without introducing the exact date. The 19th century was a time when scientific change was catching on in popular medicine like a flame on a wet log. Many doctors and scientists had been publishing findings on bacteria, spores, and viruses, and raising questions about sterile surgeries and physician cleanliness for years. The horror of the American Civil War had sadly aided in our understanding of the human body and infection. Yet, germ theory was not widely accepted until about 1890 and the health of industrial workers and coal miners was still being abused. A comprehensive safety act was not put into law in American coal mines until the late 1960s.

"The Enumerator" and "The Hall of Christmas" were just a bit of flash fiction and fun. "The Enumerator" was set in my parents' hometown. It was never meant to be a serious story, only slightly ominous. I get a kick out of it and I hope my family does too. "The Hall of Christmas" was written several years ago on Christmas Eve and read to my family for the occasion. It always seemed unfinished and I let it sit unfinished for years. I only decided to tweak the ending recently.

"Orchidaceae" is a space station of metaphors. Originally the story was meant to go in a completely different direction. I see the rock Bruno wore around his neck as the things that keep us from accepting truth; they can be shiny and nice or dull and comfortable. The orchid plant stood for truth, which we all hopefully seek—beautiful and fragile. Even before the story changed into what it became, I always knew Bruno would have to make the ultimate sacrifice for the truth.

"The First Martian" will probably be the least popular story in this collection. My poor protagonist, Rory, falls victim to morbid curiosity and prejudice. However, I think it is a good story for the anthology. If anything, "The First Martian" was written in 2019-2020, a time when truth and prejudices were being questioned more than ever before in my lifetime, and happy endings were hard to come by. I also think many wouldn't think twice about trampling alien microbes if it was in their best interests—even though other alien lifeforms could someday view us as nothing of importance and have no qualms about wiping us out.

"In Memoriam Machine" has been the best received out of all the short stories. It was even suggested that I should change the title of this collection to *In Memoriam Machine and Other Stories*. Out of all the stories in this collection, I probably spent the least amount of time on "In Memoriam Machine" because the idea had been in my head for years. My idea was to blur the line between victim and villain, and to imagine a world where you could actually walk in someone else's shoes.

I started "The Ark of the Unknown" for a bit of fun as a prequel to another yet-unpublished novel called *White Blur*, set in the same universe where the Galactic Peace Government's rule is far from peaceful. I may, at some point, return to Francis and Marco.

"Violent Messengers" was a voyage for me. First, I will address the seal. I had many who thought the seal felt out of place. I had planned to take the poor creature out of the story but was out voted by my critique group. So, the seal stayed.

Seals do occasionally get lost and make it that far inland, and by keeping it in the story it would be another way to keep with the theme of loneliness and isolation. I always wanted to write a story about how alone in the universe we feel, and I think Antarctica was a fitting setting.

I have gained so much respect for those who pour their hearts and souls into scientific research. The neutrino has always been of great interest to me. It probably started after my dad named one of our cats after the subatomic particle. I greatly respect all the effort being put into researching things many don't ever think about but that could have the greatest impact on our lives.

Acknowledgments

I want to thank my critique group, Write Club, members in the past and present, for their friendship and help, especially those who stuck it out through the pandemic. Thank you, Nathan Winfrey, for your invaluable insights, edits, and notes. Thanks, Justin Cockrell, for your edits and notes. I would like to thank my cousin, Lauren Petri, and my friend, Melanie Prengler, for their feedback on "Violent Messengers." I appreciate all my friends who read my stories and offered feedback. Thank you, Stephanie Shilling, for the wonderful cover. Thank you, Fermilab, National Science Foundation, and IceCube Neutrino Observatory, for sharing so much of your knowledge with the community. I especially want to thank Dr. John Hardin and Dr. Yuya Makino for their posts, pictures, and openness to share their overwinter experiences with the public. Thank you, Dr. Don Lincoln with Fermilab, for making physics more accessible to everyone. Thank you, National Register of Historic Places, for listing the Dawson cemetery as worthy of preservation. Thank you, Dr. Alan Derickson, for the articles and books on black lung and coal mining. I am so thankful for my family and their support. Most importantly, thank you, Sloan, for putting up with me throughout my journey with this anthology and continuing to be my best friend and partner. The stories in this anthology are fiction, and the views conveyed are my own, as are any errors, and are not to be assigned to any of the individuals or groups listed above.

R.A. Hogan grew up in Oklahoma with a passion for animals, science, and stories. She enjoyed writing from a young age. She currently lives with her husband and three dogs, writing and fostering animals for a local rescue.

www.rahoganauthor.com

Made in United States
North Haven, CT
13 July 2023

38987692R10146